I0732132

EDITED BY ALIN WALKER, MONICA LOUZON, & TIMOTHY BURKHARDT
COVER ART BY YORGOS COTRONIS

FEATURING ORIGINAL FICTION AND POETRY BY

CASSIE E. BROWN

JASON P. BURNHAM

AARON CORWIN

BRADEN FISCHER

SOPHIE GREENWOOD

HANNAH GREER

JORDAN HIRSCH

NICHOLAS JAY

JOHN PHILIP JOHNSON

RACHEL KOLAR

ANDREW KOZMA

NATHANIEL LEE

HAZELLE LERUM

AVRA MARGARITI

R. L. MEZA

MARISCA PICHETTE

CHELSEA SUTTON

GRETCHEN TESSMER

WANG CAI-YING & L. ACADIA

PUBLISHED BY THE DREAD MACHINE
www.thedreadmachine.com

ISSN APPL100002727
ISBN 978-1-957849-13-3 (Paperback)
ISBN 978-1-957849-14-0 (Epub)

Edited by Alin Walker, Monica Louzon, and Timothy Burkhardt.
Cover by Yorgos Cotronis

Published by The Dread Machine
https://www.thedreadmachine.com
Printed and bound in the United States of America.

ACKNOWLEDGMENTS

Thank you so much for reading this issue of The Dread Machine. As an independent publishing company, we sincerely appreciate your support.

This issue wouldn't have been possible without the tireless efforts of our Gatekeepers, the readers who read and rated all 1,150 submissions this quarter:

Vivian Chou
Eóin Dooley
Nathaniel Lee
Mob
Kathleen Morrish
Cody Mower
Andrew Najberg
Dan Peacock
Parker Ragland
Priya Sridhar
Kanishk Tantia
David Lee Zweifler

We'd also like to thank our Patreon supporters:
Gabe C.
Lex C.
Eric F.
Aimee H.
Akis L.
Andrew N.
Jeremy N.
Jay P.
Adrienne R.

Parker R.
Kanishk T.

If you enjoyed this issue and want to help us produce more like it, consider becoming a subscriber at thedreadmachine.com/subscribe. You can also join our Ko-fi (ko-fi.com/thedreadmachine) or Patreon (patreon.com/thedreadmachine). Every penny we receive compensates our writers and expands our library of content.

To fuel The Dread Machine in other ways, tell your friends about us. Leave reviews for our stories and issues, share our links, community, buy some stuff, or volunteer! We love making new friends!

Visit our website at www.thedreadmachine.com. You'll find links to subscribe, donate, follow, and volunteer in the footer.

Thanks again!

CONTENTS

GO WEST AND WEIRD, YOUNG WOMAN

GRETCHEN TESSMER

Shackle-Heart, the intrepid explorer
took a young wife

(at the time, she was willing)

she thought she'd see the sights
in a vast country of vaulted sky
and shimmering starlight

but soon, the air turned noxious
and someone plucked a cello string
so ominously
echoing off red mesas
resonating in salt flats

the horses were spooked
by prairie grass

sparse as it was

```
          s
          t
          o                   e
i         o     u     o       n
t         d     p     n       d
```

but Shackle-Heart was stubborn
and said, “no,
let’s keep going”

while his wife cursed the very hour he was born

until they were both weathered out
beyond speaking, trudging
in cirrus clouds of desert dust

they lost the trail and the horses
hitching the wagon
to a thirsty landscape, pockmarked by comets
and worlds colliding

death happened, as these things do

Shackle-Heart was buried with little ceremony
in the Year of Our Lord 1872

(she dug that hole with kitchen forks and a butter knife)

and all this was followed by
an unlikely, untimely

alien landing—

a glittering band of colored lights
a violin screeeeeeech of sound

sure, she'd wanted to see the sights
but this was all just…
too much, too soon

rising up from that grave
Shackle-Heart's wife was wild-eyed

chasing those spacemen off with a spoon—

"Red Devil take my husband
and Red Devil take you!"

ABOUT GRETCHEN TESSMER

Gretchen Tessmer is a writer/attorney based in the U.S.-Canadian borderlands. She writes both short fiction and poetry (so much poetry), with work appearing in over fifty publications, including Nature, Strange Horizons, Bourbon Penn, F&SF and Beneath Ceaseless Skies. Her poetry has been nominated for the Pushcart, Rhysling and Dwarf Stars awards.

GROCERY STORY

CHELSEA SUTTON

So, I'm trying to arrange the entirely fucking lackluster produce situation at New Day Foods while Lee mops the floor around me, though he seems to be pushing the dirt back and forth more than anything, rearranging the black gunk that used to be lint or hair or flecks of vegetable skin from one crack in the tile to another.

The bosses gave me crates of just-shy-of-mushy tomatoes and bananas and lettuce to arrange in some artful manner. *Artful* is the word they used. They told me to arrange the produce in such a way that any customer might be *compelled* to pick up tomatoes, bananas, and lettuce. Make them decide, shit, I need all three of those, this is what I'd been looking for my whole life.

"So, I'm looking through the dining room window, right?" says Lee. He's been talking, I realize, and I should pay attention. I'm a great multi-tasker. I'm great at juggling fucking thoughts, man, the fucking *tasks* at hand.

"Wait you're doing what?" I say.

"I'm looking through the dining room window. I'm hiding pretty good. I'm good at hiding," says Lee.

His hair looks stringy today, more than usual, almost like he collected the floor gunk and plopped that shit on his head, then sprayed it with some of that sea salt hair stuff for the wind-swept look. Hell, maybe he stood on a cliff over the ocean as part of his morning routine, I don't know what Lee *does*.

"You are very good at hiding." I'm imagining Lee's stringy head all silhouetted in some stranger's living room window and I get the chills.

"Thank you," says Lee.

"Yeah," I say.

A banana enters the shopper's life, the tomato complicates things, and lettuce wraps all that shit up in its calm and forgettable way. Everyone wants to be remembered, but not lettuce. No, that's not how lettuce plays the game. We start with something sweet but generally disappointing—the banana. Yeah, the banana comes first and then you see the tomato and you realize that what you're really missing is *passion*, man, passion that keeps life moving toward…the lettuce.

Shit, I don't know what to do.

"You don't have to try so hard. This isn't even your job," says Lee. "Sandra does the displays."

"Yeah, well, if Sandra wanted to keep this job, she shoundn'ta disappeared," I say.

"Technically," Lee continues, "it should be Billy's job when Sandra is gone, but he also disappeared."

"What's your fucking point, Lee?"

The bosses took me aside at the start of my shift and said *Hey Sammy, you took Psych in high school, you should know how to manipulate these people, move our shit into people's carts.* So it's my job now—moving this rotting shit out of here so the customers can deal with it. And customers are walking in so dead-eyed, so distracted these days, you gotta grab their attention.

"My point is, I'm looking through the window," says Lee. "And her kid, what's his name, Kimbo? Clark?" says Lee.

"How the fuck should I know?" I think I know the family Lee's going on about. They almost always come through my lane at checkout. At least the woman does.

"Kyle! It's Kyle," says Lee. "Poor little Kyle. So, it's dinnertime and they're not even sitting at the table. And they got this beautiful table, like, *gorgeous* table. You know?"

"I don't pay much attention to tables." I swap the bananas and the lettuce and that feels better for a minute. Lee is mopping hard, like really pounding at the gunk near where we used to keep the peaches, when we got deliveries of peaches. Back when we got deliveries of fresh peaches on the regular. Back when we got deliveries of anything on the regular.

"Well, it's the most beautiful table you can imagine," Lee says. "And it's dinnertime and they're not even sitting at it. Just little Kyle by himself, chomping away at some Coco Puffs, and what's-her-name and her husband are wandering around, in and out of the room, arguing about something."

"Not our business how they use their table."

"It's a waste, that's all I'm saying."

I take a step back and look at the display. The tomato is so loud in all its red.

"How does a tomato make you feel, Lee?"

"How does it make me feel?"

"Yeah, how does it make you feel?"

Lee stares at the tomato. "Nothing. Makes me feel nothing."

"If it *had* to make you feel something."

"Makes me think of spaghetti," says Lee.

"Okay."

"And blood. Lots of blood," Lee says.

"Fuck," I say.

"Sorry Sammy." Lee starts mopping again.

The word *blood* is like a flash across my brain, and all of a sudden I'm thinking back to yesterday. I was getting gas on my way to work, and I go to use the bathroom. It was locked and had been locked for a while, so the clerk and I broke in to see what's up, and there was a guy in there who'd died. I can't say how, exactly. But there was blood everywhere, fucking—what's the word?—*tendrils* of blood hanging off the walls. He'd been there most of the afternoon and no one noticed. And there was this smell in the room, I don't even know how to describe it. But familiar. Like something from the back of the refrigerator.

And after I peed in the field behind the gas station, I sat in my car and just sorta stared into space. I mean, physically that's what I was doing, but really my mind was on the body. On the blood. Anyway, I couldn't sit there staring all damn day and wait for the cops. I couldn't afford another late penalty.

"So, I'm looking through the window," says Lee, "and Kyle isn't much of an eater. He's as thin as a celery stick, so I just watch what's-her-name and her husband—"

"Carol," I say.

"What?"

"That's her name, I think. Or Cathy." She wouldn't be noteworthy except that she has a premium rewards card, and the bosses always require us to repeat the name of the premium rewards shopper that pops up on the screen. *Thanks for being a New Day Foods loyal shopper, Carol. (Or Cathy.)*

"Connie?" Lee is searching his brain.

"Maybe. Maybe that. That sounds right."

"You should know. You gotta pay attention," says Lee.

"I fucking pay attention," I say.

"So, I'm watching Connie or Cathy and her husband move from kitchen to hallway to living room and to rooms I can't see, but I can still hear 'em. I couldn't make out the words, just a weird uneasy mix of shouting and whispering, mixing so much it's like they're swallowing each other's words—*swallowing*—and there's little Kyle, just munching at the chocolate cereal, which is really no excuse for a dinner, if you ask me."

I've moved the tomato a bit further away from the bananas, but now I'm worrying about the dick-to-balls comparison ratio and if I'm going to be fired for accidentally creating a pornographic display with produce. "How does the tomato make you feel now?" I ask Lee.

"Stop obsessing over the tomato. I'm trying to tell you something."

"I don't want to hear about you stalking people anymore." I shouldn't have said that but it's hard, being a multitasker and keeping an eye on every little *feeling.*

"I'm not stalking! It's research!" says Lee.

Sure. Following customers home is totally normal and not a lead-up to murder. That's what I think and have been thinking, and I go ahead and say it.

"Take that back. It's not even funny," says Lee. "I got a gift of memory, Sammy, and what good is a gift if you don't use it, huh?"

Yeah, maybe I got a gift too, maybe I'm a rare talent, and maybe I like my job but sometimes I sit in the parking lot after my shift, when I suddenly don't have a purpose or a next thing on my list and the evening is stretching out ahead of me like a desert and I think, *well, that was cute and all, but what's the point?* The thing is, it's not the job that makes me think that. I'm pretty sure if I was a doctor or lawyer or superhero, I'd sit there too. Staring.

And thinking about that body I saw yesterday.

The guy had been gnawed on and spit out all over. I know food. My job is food and I can tell when someone's chewed on an apple or something and not paid for it. Happens all the time. Take a bite out of something, decide it isn't for you, and stuff it back where you found it, good side out, so it takes ages for anyone to notice.

I can't be in the produce section anymore, now that I'm thinking of people taking bites out of my tomatoes and not paying for them. I head to the canned food aisle, Lee trailing behind me, whispering at my back the whole way.

"I remember what the customers get every week and I start seeing the patterns, like some detective in those old black and white movies," he's saying, and I've heard some of this shit before. I try to keep my mind focused on what he's saying and the task at hand, since I got a lot of tasks, since I'm so trusted here, a real employee-of-the-month type.

And Lee goes on: "Every night I smoke and pace and try to piece out what they're probably having for dinner, based on what they bought here that day. And I started going to the customers' houses as a way to...just confirm. You gotta confirm things, Sammy."

Canned food. Peas, kidney beans, chicken soup.

"I just peek in their window," says Lee, "try to see what they're eating. Or I poke through the trash cans—food packages, rotten leftovers, scraps from cooking—all paints a picture. You know, I got so good, I can predict what they're going to buy the *next* time they come here. I'm just confirming reality is reality."

Peas, kidney beans, chicken soup. *Sell these Sammy*, the bosses said. *Let them deal with the expiration dates and the rotting.*

There's no story here. Kidney beans are kinda red, but a sad red. Not a passionate red. And there is nothing like the smell of kidney beans rotting in your fridge. Like death. "What's the use if I can't confirm that I'm right, you know?" says Lee. "What's the point? Here I am thinking I'm good at something, but if I never take the chance to see for sure—to see I'm really right about it all—what's it even matter? If I can't prove it, it's not real, and it's gotta be real, Sammy."

Kidney beans. That's what the guy in the bathroom smelled like. Rotting kidney beans half digested, the bile of something eating but not filling up, not absorbing anything.

"You're not listening," says Lee.

"I'm a multitasker," I say. "You can't always tell, but I'm multitasking."

"So, I watched Connie or Cathy fight with the husband," says Lee, "and poor little Kyle eating his chocolate cereal. I watch for a long time, and not one pan goes on the stove, not one box of pasta opened, not one chicken put in the oven. Yesterday was trash day, so the empty bins don't give me any clues to the rest of the week. The whole trip was for nothing. All I got was muddy knees and a knotted-up stomach. I didn't learn a damn thing about how they're using the food they're buying."

I arrange the cans. Peas. Then soup. Then beans. Beans seem to be the finale here.

"Lee, I'm thinking maybe you should…get a different hobby," I say. My voice is shaking and I don't know why. There's a customer wandering down the aisle toward us and I'm trying to focus on the task at hand and get the display looking good by the time she gets close enough to see.

"Don't you wonder about people though?" says Lee. "Like, they're buying tomatoes but how many of those tomatoes are going to rot on the counter? How many bowls of rice will get thrown in the trash? How many gallons of milk will get chunky?"

"That's not my job. My job is to get them to buy it. Not my business what they do after. You can be a student of the people without going through their garbage." Just another minute. She's walking real slowly, aimless, like she didn't bring a list, so this display really has to *pop*.

"But that's the only way," says Lee. "People show you who they are by what they throw away."

"And by what they *buy*." I switch the beans and the peas. Yeah. Maybe we gotta be brutal here. The kidney beans right off the bat. I can almost smell them through the can and I feel queasy. No no no no— soup first, beans last.

Shit.

Lee looks at the display. "It's fine," he says.

Fucking *fine?*

The woman is here, almost runs right into Lee and his mop, and I think maybe she's not even going to notice my work, so I'm holding my breath because I don't want her to notice *me*, I want her to notice the *soup*. And then she stops and lingers, and she grabs the kidney beans, the fucking *beans*, and drops the can into her cart.

Lee is talking but I don't hear him because I'm a little pissed she didn't grab the soup first like I'd planned, but then I'm watching her walk away and *I swear to fuck* she's got a bite out of her shoulder and there's blood dripping down her blouse. And the smell—

"I'm not done yet with the story," says Lee.

"Do you see that," I say, pointing at the blouse.

"You never listen to me," says Lee.

"Are you seeing *that*?" I try to turn Lee's shoulders toward the woman but he doesn't like being touched, and he pushes back and his mop clocks me in the shoulder and I fall into the display, the cans slamming to the linoleum and rolling all over. One of the beans pops open and leaks where Lee had been mopping. And I can smell it, like the beans have turned.

Lee doesn't look at me, just starts mopping it up and mumbling *I'm sorry I'm sorry.*

My shoulder's aching where the mop handle knocked me, but the woman turned the corner of the aisle. I stumble stupidly over the rolling cans of beans and soup and peas to try to flag her down, so I can say *hey, I think you're bleeding. And those beans might be expired. Excuse me, loyal New Day Foods shopper, I think you have a bite out of your flesh.*

I look down the next two aisles but she's nowhere.

The store has been so empty lately, maybe I'm just making up customers now.

I keep on going to the meat aisle for the last display. Chicken, beef, pork. Lee follows me, mopping the floors where the weird meat grease drips off the packages, like a butcher-mutant's saliva or some shit.

Now move this dead flesh, Sammy, the bosses said. *Don't make their deaths mean nothing. Don't let their deaths be pointless.* Nothing worse than that, if you ask me, something dies with no purpose but to sit and slowly expire, stinking up the whole damn place.

Chicken, cow, pig. Have to think about this one.

"I'm sorry," says Lee.

"I'm trying to *think*," I say.

Lee's breathing right behind me, and if I thought he was a real threat to anyone, maybe I'd be uncomfortable. But it's not Lee we gotta be afraid of in this world.

"Maybe you need something flashy for this. More than a sign," Lee says. "Wrap it up like a gift. Ribbons or something." He starts mopping slowly around the meat display, trying to catch every drip.

That's actually a good idea. I head to the break room, Lee following, his mop dragging the meat saliva all over, but I try not to think about it, disease trailing on the floor everywhere I go. The break room is empty, coffee from yesterday still burning in the pot, the fridge left open a little bit, something moist and chunky sliding out of the drawer and onto the floor.

Lee mops that up too, as I dig through the party supply cabinet and find some red ribbon from Sandra's birthday a couple months ago.

"So, that all happened last night," says Lee, mopping and following, "at the house with Connie or Cathy and Kyle and the cereal. And so this morning, I overhear some old ladies buying English muffins and marmalade saying there'd been a disturbance last night, real late. That's what they called it. A *disturbance* on Laurel Street, and everyone's gone, that's all they said, just like all the others, just that everyone was *gone*, and they're giggling and sighing over their English muffins but not saying why there are people disappearing, not saying why everyone is gone or what that even means. And I can't ask because I don't want them knowing I'm listening. And I get this bad feeling."

I have to pee, I realize, and I glance over at the employee bathroom in the corner of the break room but the door is closed and that little red OCCUPIED slider is clicked over and I don't want to knock on a locked bathroom ever again. I'll hold it.

I walk back to the meats, Lee following and yammering on. I make him hold onto an end of ribbon so I can cut it precisely, because this matters, this is going to be fucking *gorgeous*, this display, and the bow is going to *work*.

"So, I take my first break this morning as soon as I can, and I go back to the house," says Lee. "There's police tape on the front door but not really any cops, just one sitting in their car staring off into nothing. And there are a couple neighbors sitting in their cars too, or standing real still on their porches, just looking out at nothing. I don't even think they see me walk up the sidewalk."

The ribbon is looking fucking gorgeous.

"So, I go to the dining room window," says Lee, "exactly where I was sitting the night before, and the cereal bowl little Kyle was eating from was still there. Not sure why he wouldn't have put it in the sink when he was done eating, but some kids are raised different. I couldn't see anyone moving around, and what I got concerned about, actually, is the gallon of milk she bought a couple days before. If they're all gone now, I mean, I'm sure little Kyle didn't drink the whole gallon in his Coco Puffs, so all I can think about is the milk sitting in their fridge, slowly going sour. Milk only lasts for what? A week? Two weeks? Who knows how long they're going to be gone. I just had this terrible vision of the milk going all rotten and eating through its plastic jug and then eating through the shelves, and at that point, *who knows* what kind of damage milk can do."

"This is really coming together," I say, stepping back to admire the ribbons and the goddamn *celebration of life* happening for this meat right here. I'm so *proud* of myself, I never get to feel *proud.*

"So, I break into the house," says Lee.

"You what now?" I say.

"I break in because I'm afraid of the milk, you see."

"The cops didn't see you?"

"I told you. Everyone was just staring into space, not paying attention. You gotta pay attention, Sammy, this is what I *mean.* I just walked in the back door. Not really breaking and entering when you just *enter.*"

I think I hear the squeaky wheel of a cart behind us. I spin thinking maybe it's the woman with the bite and the beans but no one's there.

"So, I go to the kitchen to get the milk," says Lee. "I'm just thinking of them. I'm just trying to take care of them."

I'm getting this gnawing feeling, like right before the gas station clerk and I broke down that door, like there's something I shouldn't be seeing, that I should just keep ignoring, find a different fucking bathroom, leave the milk alone, focus on the task at hand.

"But the floors are sticky," says Lee. "All the floors, everywhere. All covered in this red gunk. There's red everywhere. Like tomato sauce. But I know Connie or Cathy doesn't *ever* buy tomato sauce, Sammy. I know because I pay attention. I *remember*."

"What was it then?" I ask. I'm looking around the store. I think there are footsteps somewhere. Fuck. Is that another wheel? Is that breathing?

"It was blood. Blood in long trails, like they were just bleeding and walking around. Bleeding, walking around, something gnawing on them, slowly stringing out their insides. Blood like ribbons all over the house."

I think I hear chewing. Or was it there the whole time? Why wasn't I paying attention?

"So, I try not to step on the red stuff but there's so much of it. I go get the milk. But there were other things in there—stuff that would go bad. Some fruit. A head of lettuce. Bananas on the counter. I just took it all. So it wouldn't stink. So it would be okay for them when they came back."

The ribbon is fucking perfect. But it doesn't matter because in between Lee's words, I can hear the bathroom door in the break room click. I can hear the fucking hinges cry out as the door opens.

"Blood like ribbons everywhere," Lee says. "I left the canned goods because they'll be okay. Canned goods don't bother themselves with much. Canned goods will be fine."

There's a growl somewhere, but I can't tell if it's my stomach or the meat coolers popping on or if it's coming from the break room. Or something else fucking entirely. This had been a good day, too.

"You know what the real kicker of the whole Connie or Cathy thing is, though?" says Lee. "I'm never gonna know if I was right about the dinner she was going to make that night. It's too bad. I was on a roll."

Lee keeps mopping, but I hold steady as I see the customer with the kidney beans appear from an aisle, her eyes suddenly wide open, just like mine, holding still except for her good arm reaching up slowly to touch the bite, like she was just noticing it, like she wasn't *paying attention* before. We stand there, like the three of us are some kind of display, waiting for whatever the footsteps and the growls belong to, whatever is emerging from the break room, needing us to tell it what it needs, what it's hungry for, what it's been looking for its whole life.

ABOUT CHELSEA SUTTON

Chelsea Sutton is an LA-based writer and director of speculative stories. She was a 2016 PEN America Emerging Voices Fellow and an alum of the 2022 Clarion UCSD Science Fiction and Fantasy Workshop, and her fiction has appeared in *Bourbon Penn, F(riction), Speculative City, CRAFT Literary, Luna Station Quarterly, Orca Literary*, and the new anthology *Mooncalves*, among others. Also a playwright, she was a Humanitas PlayLA award winner and her macabre steampunk adaptation of Pinocchio, *Wood Boy Dog Fish*, appeared in the inaugural season at the Garry Marshall Theatre. She co-wrote *Welcome to the Blumhouse Live*, an interactive film event for Blumhouse/Amazon Prime by Little Cinema, which was nominated for a 2021 Emmy for Outstanding Interactive Program. She holds an MFA from UC Riverside. Chelseasutton.com

Originally published by Podcastle, March 2021.

#BLOODBOSSBABES

RACHEL KOLAR

Hey Girl!
From: Amy Shearer (serpentsisteramy@sotesh.com)
To: Heather McBride (mcheather@ymail.com)

Hey, girlfriend! Love looking at your beautiful family on Insta. And congrats on getting into grad school—that's HUGE!

Furthering your education while raising a family takes so much dedication, and that's why I think you'd be AMAZING on my team. For the past six months, I've been offering blood libations to Sotesh, Mother of Serpents, and let me tell you, it has changed my life! I get to set my own schedule, bleeding the unbelievers when it's convenient for me. I have the security of knowing that when Sotesh comes in Her glory, I'll be spared the worst of Her wrath. And She gives Her believers THE BEST gifts! Just last week, I hit Green Level and was blessed with the ability to shed my soft warm-blood skin. Check out these before and after pics—my acne is COMPLETELY gone! #CobraClear #WhiteheadsAreForWarmbloods

I'm looking to pick up some acolytes, and you'd be a natural. Let me know if you're interested! And give my love to Jason and the kids. <3
XOXOXO,
Amy

Re: Re: Hey Girl!
From: Amy Shearer (serpentsisteramy@sotesh.com)
To: Heather McBride (mcheather@ymail.com)

LOLOL! No no nooooooo, the Sisterhood of Sotesh is NOT a demonic murder cult. Murder is ILLEGAL and I would never be part of something like that. I don't know where Jason gets those ideas! He must have heard about groups like the Order of the Bleeding Maw. *They're* a demonic murder cult, and they make legitimate religions like the Sisterhood look bad. We're just a badass network of women empowering women to empower the Devourer of All Flesh.

Jason should be all for this, though, because joining the Sisterhood will help your whole family! I know how lonely the mom thing can be, and it's been SUCH a support for me to have all these awesome blood boss babes on my side. You can't take care of the fam if you can't take care of yourself, right mama? Plus, your blood libations can earn all sorts of treats and blessings for the kiddos! My little Paisleigh just started tasting the air, and baking cookies with her has never been so fun.

Let me know when you're ready to make your first sacrifice!

XOXOXO,
Amy

Re: Just a few questions
From: Amy Shearer (serpentsisteramy@sotesh.com)
To: Heather McBride (mcheather@ymail.com)

Hey girl! You are SO SMART to ask all these questions—this is why I've always admired you. <3

I had a lot of questions at first, too, but joining was SO worth it. I remember what my Sunday mornings used to look like—running around, putting the kids in clothes that they hated, and ignoring them for an hour, right? And they couldn't play soccer because of all the Sunday morning games. But with Sotesh, I get to set my own worship hours, and all that is over! I wouldn't trade the friends Paisleigh and Jaxtyn made in soccer for anything. #GoHuntsvilleHatchlings

And it's not just the scheduling, it's the peace of mind. I go to sleep every night knowing that when Sotesh comes in Her glory, my fam won't be devoured in flames along with the other soft-skins. What kind of mama would I be if I couldn't shed a few drops for my kiddos' futures?

Tell you what, you take all the time you need to think about it. You're a smart lady, and I know you'll be happy no matter what you choose!

XOXOXO,
Amy

Serpent Sistahs!
From: Amy Shearer (serpentsisteramy@sotesh.com)
To: Heather McBride (mcheather@ymail.com)

EEEEEEEEEEEEEK! OMG, I'm SO EXCITED to have you on board, hun! You are going to ROCK this!

I've attached everything you need for your first libation. I know a pint sounds like a lot, but really, it's what the Red Cross takes, and people donate blood all the time, right? And even if you decide the Sisterhood isn't for you, your sacrifice still gets you those bitching fangs, and you don't HAVE to use them to drain blood for Her Dark Majesty. They're great for cutting through packing tape. And hey . . . Jason might find some fun uses for them, hot stuff!

One other important thing: Sotesh demands a libation on the night of each full moon. But good news—it doesn't have to come from you! Go on social media and let everyone know how much the Sisterhood has changed your life, and your friends will be begging to throw in a pint! And you can always ask a gal pal out for coffee and see if she'll let you bite her at the end of the date. If she's a real friend, she'll be happy to open her veins in praises of Her All-Devouring Magnificence.

Welcome aboard, serpent sistah!

XOXOXO,
Amy

Re: FIRST SACRIFICE!!!!!
From: Amy Shearer (serpentsisteramy@sotesh.com)
To: Heather McBride (mcheather@ymail.com)

EEEEEEEEEEEEEEEK! OMG, you are SMASHING your goals like the skulls of Sotesh's prey! Don't knock it, sister—a tablespoon is nothing to sneeze at, and I just KNOW that it's the first of many to come!

About banking it until the next full moon: noooo! It *sounds* like a good idea, but the smart thing is to invest it in blessings from the Great One. Once you've gained more of Her gifts, you'll *really* get those libations pouring out. Just a few more tablespoons and you'll have half a cup, which gets you those GORGEOUS golden slit-pupil eyes. The minute somebody sees them, they'll be dying to hear about how Sotesh has changed your life! Or if you REALLY want to treat yourself, you can pour out another pint and get the power to perform a sinuous, mesmeric dance. Can you *imagine* how you'll be able to bring the blood cascading in when you can entice your prey like that?

I know you only have a tablespoon for now, but if you have to, you can put in just a little more from yourself until more comes in. Because more *is* coming in! Believe in Sotesh, and She'll believe in you!

XOXOXO,
Amy

Re: Coffee
From: Amy Shearer (serpentsisteramy@sotesh.com)
To: Heather McBride (mcheather@ymail.com)

Ugh, no offense, but your sister sounds like a total neg-ferret! I can't BELIEVE she isn't supporting you! Your body makes half again as much blood when you're pregnant, so it's not like she can't spare a cup. I HATE when stupid cows like that won't support other women!

Deep breaths, mama. You can do this before the full moon gets here! And even if you can't—and that's a big if!—it won't hurt to bleed yourself once, right? Just while you build up your base. Everybody has to do that sometimes—it's no big.

Speaking of your base: I know you're working the one-time libations, but have you been recruiting acolytes? Every new member of the Sisterhood helps to hasten the glorious coming of Sotesh, and some of the blood from your acolytes' libations gets credited to you, so you don't have to gather so much. Plus you get the coolest perks when you convert unbelievers! You saw my sweet Green Level scales. And only acolytes of Pink Level or higher will get thralls of our own when She comes in Her glory!

Go out and get bleeding. You've got this!

XOXOXO,
Amy

Re: Worried
From: Amy Shearer (serpentsisteramy@sotesh.com)
To: Heather McBride (mcheather@ymail.com)

I am not loving your attitude. Or Jason's attitude. I really think you're letting his negativity affect you. Look, I know the full moon is tomorrow, but *it's one full moon.* It won't kill you to give a pint of your own this once. And while we're at it, I know you already shed for the golden eyes and the starter fangs, but why didn't you pony up for hibernation powers instead of the unhinging jaw? Another pint wouldn't feel like so much if you could sleep for a week after.

Look, it's hard, but stay positive. Put on your makeup, drink your coffee, and *don't let anyone tell you that you look pale.* Pale is a state of mind, hun! Remember, "ANEMIA" stands for "Allowing Negative Energy to Muzzle Ideas and Actions." Anyone who says you're pale is a jealous hater trying to drag you down, and if there's one thing Sotesh can't stand, it's haters. Just keep smiling and telling everyone how great the eyes and the jaw are. When they see how happy you are, they'll want to get in on it, too. Fake it till you make it, blood boss babe!

And seriously, *stop listening to Jason.* Whatever you need to do to get that negativity out of your life, do it. You don't want Sotesh blaming you or the kids for his mood-hoovering, do you?

XOXOXO,
Amy

Re: Second Thoughts
From: Amy Shearer (serpentsisteramy@sotesh.com)
To: Heather McBride (mcheather@ymail.com)

No no no no nooooooo, *I did not tell you to pony up for hibernation powers right now.* I said that IF YOU HAD DONE IT BEFORE, you'd be fine. OF COURSE now you don't have enough blood left for tonight, not even if you hibernate after. FFS, did you even read the welcome packet?

Look, you have everything going for you right now. You're up to four powers! You should be getting sacrifices by the gallon! Stop blaming me and Sotesh for your bad choices. If you blame anyone, it should be Jason for not supporting you in your new life.

Work it out. Do whatever you need to do. *Whatever you need to do.* Or Sotesh will be PISSED.

XOXOXO,
Amy

Re: Heather
From: Amy Shearer (mawmama@ootbm.com)
To: Jen Bradshaw (jenniferbradshaw89@woohoo.com)

Hey girl!

So good to hear from you! OMG, I couldn't believe when I heard about Heather, either. And no, *of course* I didn't tell her to bleed her husband to death! Some people just aren't cut out for the religious life.

It's sad.

I mean, it doesn't help that the Sisterhood of Sotesh was kind of a racket. They're supposed to be all about sisterhood, but a snake is kind of phallic for that, amiright? Plus Sotesh's infernal gifts are total crap. I won't lie, I followed her for, like, five minutes, but my left fang broke right away. Lame.

I'm so lucky I've found a *real* religion. Have you heard about the Order of the Bleeding Maw? I've just joined, and it's been a life changer. Forget about all that Sotesh anemia nonsense—when blood drips out of your family's mouths 24/7, you always know where to find more if you're running low! And I'm never going to need to buy lipstick again, which is amaaaaaaaaazing for my budget.

I'm super glad you reached out, because I'm looking for a new acolyte to join my team. Let me know if you're interested—you'd be a natural!

XOXOXO,
Amy

ABOUT RACHEL KOLAR

Rachel Kolar is the author of *Mother Ghost: Nursery Rhymes for Little Monsters*, and her fiction for adults has appeared in *Podcastle*, *Metaphorosis*, *Crossed Genres*, and several other professional and semipro zines. A graduate of Kenyon College, Rachel lives with her husband and children in the Baltimore/Washington area, where they enjoy hiking, playing overly complicated board games, and plotting new ways to terrorize trick-or-treaters. You can follow Rachel on Tumblr at @RachelKolar, on Facebook at RachelKolarspecfic, or on Mastodon at RachelKolar@wandering.shop

THE INNOCENT JAR

NATHANIEL LEE

The first thing you have to understand is that my apartment is way too big, and I'm kind of a clutterbug, so I lose stuff constantly. I've got three bedrooms and two bathrooms, and it's just me living here. I don't know what I was thinking when I moved in. Half the rooms I don't even use; they're just full of random junk and collectibles: old furniture, clothes, knick-knacks and gewgaws. I like to rummage through antique stores and pawn shops and garage sales. My motto is: you never know when you might need something. For instance, I live in a land-locked city, but I have an inflatable raft under my bed. King-size, because I like to stretch out. I've got a baby swing, a crib, and a bundle of infant clothes all stacked up in a corner behind the dining room table; I'm sure as hell not using those any time soon, unless I learn how to reproduce asexually, but I have them (just in case). There's an old plow yoke that lives in the coat closet, behind the two coats I actually use. I think I was planning on doing a rustic decoration theme at some point? Hard to remember, but when I do, I'll be prepared.

The main point is that it's not unusual for me to misplace things or find something I can't remember obtaining in the first place.

I like the crowded, slapdash arrangement I have, the amusing surprises and helpful coincidences, and normally I'm pretty blasé about losing things (I've got fifteen of everything I'd ever need—and the fun is in the finding and the getting, not the having), but the other day, I was having the worst sense of... deja vu, I guess? Some kind of obsessive disorder, maybe.

I had a vision in my head of a jar, a very particular jar. Light blue ceramic, a couple of handles on the sides, and a little lid on top that I knew would open with a pop, because it had a cork stopper. Almost like an urn. Nothing special, really. I had no idea where I would have gotten it or why, and I really wasn't sure why I wanted to find it so badly, but I became convinced that it was somewhere in my apartment, and I couldn't rest until I found it.

I tore apart the kitchen, two of the bedrooms, and most of the living room, opening drawers and dumping out old spectacles, silver state-crest spoons, costume jewelry, an old set of manacles. I found a stash of old mezzotints in frames and a really nice top hat, a big brass doorknob with matching key, a cashmere scarf, and a set of My Little Pony toys from the eighties. I even found a folder of schoolwork, elementary school stuff (not mine; no idea where that even would have come from). But I didn't find that jar.

Finally, I sat on the floor amid a haphazard sprawl of vinyl records and cassettes, stewing over my failure. I wanted the jar so badly I could taste it (dusty and dry, like the ghost of mildew). And then I realized how absurd I looked, pouting in the middle of the mess I'd made of my toys like an overgrown toddler, and I started laughing. I thought about calling out for a pizza, but I was feeling a little claustrophobic. I decided to go out.

Later, as I was walking home full of kebabs and a couple of beers, I spotted a junk shop I didn't recognize. This, you might imagine, is a pretty rare experience for someone of my inclinations.

The inside of the shop was startlingly brightly lit. You think of those places as having a couple of thirty-watts flickering in dusty shades at best, but this one was as well-lit as a big box store, harsh light that threw tiny, ink-black circles of shadow on the floor under every object. The man behind the counter caught my eye as I entered and smiled, big and wide. It was like he recognized me, but not as a friend. More like a dealer seeing his number one pillhead rolling up on payday.

"Welcome back," he said. "You look like a man with a burden upon his life."

I'd never seen him before. He had the kind of face your eyes slide off of, could be anywhere between twenty-five and fifty, a middling skin tone that could have come from anyplace on three continents, a precise but empty accent that revealed exactly nothing. The stuff in the shop looked pretty standard—musty books here, vintage radios there, old clothes in the middle, and some spindly chairs in the back. I was losing my beer buzz and starting to feel disappointed.

That's when I saw it behind the counter. Pale blue, like a robin's egg. Two small handles. Round stoppered lid. The jar, the one in my head. Here, in this random rubbish-filled store that I'd never heard of.

I came up to the counter, but my mouth was too dry. I licked my lips and pointed, wide-eyed, at the jar.

"Ah, you hear it calling?" The shopkeep smiled. "But that is a lie, as it is a lie."

"How much?" I managed. "For the jar?"

He laughed. "The Innocent Jar? It is worthless. But for what is inside, I think, for you, a bargain can be made."

I blinked. It was hard not to look at the jar. "What do you mean? What's inside it?"

He looked side to side as though checking for spies, then leaned in and gestured me closer. "Nothing!" he whispered gleefully, and laughed again. More of a cackle.

"How much?" I snapped.

"It does not matter," he said, shrugging with one shoulder. "Let us say... fifty dollars."

I already had my wallet out and slapped a fifty onto the counter. He caught my hand like a gecko snapping a cricket and held it down. "I think this will be the last time I tell you this," he said, "but it must be done. It must be done correctly. *Innocent*, from *nocere*, meaning *to harm*, and *in-*, meaning *without*. *Nocere* from the older root, *nek*." He stared at me and his eyes were clear like glass. "*Nek* is death. *In-nek*. Deathless. Eternity." He glanced to the side, and I saw the jar had moved to the countertop when I wasn't looking. "The vessel is empty, do you understand? It has always been empty and it always will be empty. No matter what you put in, there will never be anything there, and you will never receive anything back. Nothing comes out of the jar," he tightened his grip and I tried to pull away, "because there is *nothing* inside the jar."

He released my hand so abruptly that I stumbled backwards. The next coherent memory I have is of walking down the street to the subway station, feeling the chill of the autumn night and the even colder lump of the Innocent Jar cradled in my left arm. My hand still stung where the shopkeep's fingernails had dug in.

He'd called me a man with a burden on my life. What the hell did that even mean? I pushed open the door to my apartment building and started up the stairs. Burdens, though. I used to have friends. College friends, work friends. Everyone has friends. But then... people drift. Everyone couples up and settles down, has children and mortgages and career paths and two weeks of vacation (if they're lucky). No more time. But I'm free. Free and easy.

By the time I got home, I felt like I'd swallowed a rock. Kebab meat must have been off. I went to sit down, but the couch was covered with half-tumbled boxes. I groaned and leaned over, placing the blue jar gently onto the cushions before I rested my hands on the couch's arm and back and breathed through my nose. I smelled dust and dry wood and old paper, normally some of my favorite things, but they just made things worse. I sat onto the floor with a grunt. The jar tipped to the side and I gasped in horror, scrabbling to catch it before it fell, before she fell and hurt herself.

The chill of the hardened clay in my hands reminded me that I hadn't opened the jar yet. He'd said it was empty.

The lid resisted at first, but after a gentle twist, it slid out like it had been greased. I couldn't see inside the jar. I turned it to face the light from the window. Still nothing. Dark as the bottom of the sea. I pulled the lampshade off of... it must have been a lamp, on the side table. The blackness inside didn't move or react even as I moved the... the light source closer to it.

But the lamp is gone. It went into the jar, but the jar is empty, and I can't remember what I had been holding. It was... not. It had never been. I only know it was a lamp because the shade is still here. I can't remember what it looked like, let alone where I found it or how long I'd had it or what its story had been.

I set the jar down very, very carefully and put the lid on top like I was deactivating a landmine. I had most of a bottle of whiskey in the kitchen, so I proceeded to get extremely drunk while I tried to absorb the idea that I had some kind of portable black hole in a cheery, baby-blue jug. A memory hole. An oubliette. (French word. Means "forgotten." It's a type of dungeon, like a well. A deep pit with a door at the top. You throw people in and they never come out.)

Around about two a.m., the whiskey ran out. I sat in the dark without a lamp and cradled the jar on my lap like a child, like my little girl. I looked at the mess I still hadn't cleaned up and suddenly I was angry. I had all the time in the world to myself, nothing to do and nowhere to go, and all I'd done was collect all this stuff. This junk, this garbage, this fucking *clutter*. My burden. That's what he'd meant. I was wasting my time on all these *things* that I didn't even want.

I started slow. Rolled up clothes and poked them in, probably tossed the hangers in after, left empty closets. I know there used to be books on these shelves, there must have been, so those had gone in. At some point, I must have experimented with its capacity for size, because parts of the couch are missing, things far too big to have ever fit through the jar's tiny mouth, let alone inside it. But there is nothing in the jar, and there never will be, and nothing is infinite. Nothing is eternal. After this I'd be free as a bird, naked and flying forever.

Things... got a little crazy. The two bedrooms I mentioned before? I didn't bring up the third, because it's completely empty, and I have no idea what used to be in it. Well, no, that's a lie, ha-ha, I know exactly what was in it; nothing, because whatever was there, I put in the jar, and—there is *nothing* in the jar.

It's early morning now and I stopped because I found something in the empty room, and it stopped me. I haven't put it in the jar. Not yet.

It's a photograph. A pretty new one, in a frame and everything, but the glass is cracked, so it must have been under something. It shows a man and a woman, a little girl who looks about eight and another child about two or three, laughing and smiling for the camera. They're on a beach. There's a boat in the background. I don't recognize any of the people in it.

No, that's a lie too. The man has my face. He has my face and his arm around this woman and he's smiling too, but I don't recognize him at all, except for one thing. His eyes. His eyes look like my eyes, now, in the mirror in the hall bathroom, with the Innocent Jar sitting on the toilet bowl beside me. He looks tired. He looks frustrated and chained. He looks like he is lying. He looks like he's got a burden on his life.

The man at the store, he'd said "welcome back." He said this would be the last time. What did I do? What did I put in the jar, the other time I had it? Or was it *times*? Did they go one by one, or all at once? Did they fight? Did they even know it was happening, that it had happened before? How much of their lives had I poured into that endless, infinite dark before I stopped being able to remember or imagine why I had a crib, a folder of schoolwork, a woman's cashmere scarf?

Oubliette has the same root as *oblivion*. *Innocent* can mean *unknowing*. I am sitting here with half of my life missing and I don't know how much more, and the jar is beside me. It's cold. It's always cold on the outside of the jar. Will it be as cold inside, in the dark? I don't think so. I think it will be warm, like a nice bath at the end of a hard day. How much of me will go in before that stops mattering? To me? To anyone?

I don't know if this will survive. I don't know if you will believe it. It was written by no one, after all.

Because there is nothing inside the jar. Nothing at all.

ABOUT NATHANIEL LEE

Nate lives in Oregon and is frequently rained upon. He puts words into various orders. Occasionally people give him money for this. No one knows why. You can read his writing and find links to his published works at www.mirrorshards.net.

OLD MOTHER GNOME

AVRA MARGARITI

We feed her sorrows:
The time the priest's
Hands wandered too
Close to our dress collars,
Or when our fathers
Reminisced bearing witness
To the burning of witches;
When our school teacher
Whipped our bare skin bloody
For daring to kiss each
Other's chapped lips.

Old Mother Gnome
Fractures her jaw wide
Enough to encompass
Our matchstick bodies.
There's joy in devouring,

She says, in keeping children
Safe from the world.

And we all hold hands
Like wilting daisy chains
So as not to lose each other

On our way down the larynx
Of Old Mother Gnome,
Her hot-spring stomach acid
A balm to our weary,
Still-growing bones.
When I give birth to you,
Her voice quakes and rumbles,
It will be a new era,
And you the child rulers

Heralding its dawn.

ABOUT AVRA MARGARITI

Avra Margariti is a queer Social Work undergrad from Greece. She enjoys storytelling in all its forms and writes about diverse identities and experiences. Their work has appeared or is forthcoming in *Flash Fiction Online*, *The Forge Literary*, *The Journal of Compressed Creative Arts*, *SmokeLong Quarterly*, and other venues. Avra won the 2019 Bacopa Literary Review prize for fiction. You can find them on Twitter @avramargariti.

Originally published on Tor.com, March 2023.

BRIMSTONE AND MARMALADE

AARON CORWIN

Mathilde didn't want a demon. She wanted a pony.

"Ponies are expensive," Mathilde's mother said. "How about a nice little demon instead?"

"I don't want a demon!" Mathilde stamped her foot. "Demons are ugly and creepy and they smell bad!"

"Ponies are hard work," Mathilde's father said. "You wouldn't have time for your homework."

"I would!" Mathilde said. "I'd work really hard and take good care of him!"

"Well," Father said. "We'll see."

Mathilde knew what "we'll see" meant. It was one of those special lies that only grown-ups were allowed to tell. When a grown-up said "we'll see," it really meant "never."

It wasn't fair. Becky Hamilton got to take riding lessons on weekends, and she never stopped talking about them.

Peter Voorhees brought his demon to school once. It was scaly and slobbery, not sleek and pretty like a pony. It got loose in the classroom and tried to eat Mathilde's hair.

How could anyone think that a demon was better than a pony?

———

The day before Mathilde's birthday in September, the sky was gray and drizzly all afternoon and the puddles swirled with little flat rainbows. On that day, something different happened.

"Mathilde?" That was Mrs. Pressmorton, the vice principal. Mathilde looked up from the floor, one galosh halfway onto her foot.

"Mathilde, your parents called to say you don't have to take the bus home today. Your grandmother is picking you up from school."

Mathilde's heart began to beat faster. Nana? She thought. Nana's here for my birthday?

She tried not to hope. She tried so, so hard, but little bits of hope started to creep in anyway. Nana always brought presents, even when it wasn't her birthday. And—and this was the deepest, most secret hope of all—Nana lived in the big house in the country; the big house with the old barn and the great big field.

"Oh my goodness!" Nana said. She swept Mathilde up in a great big hug, just like she always did.

"Nana!" Mathilde definitely didn't peer over Nana's shoulder, looking for a pony in the back of her car. Not much, anyway.

"Look at you!" Nana said. "My little Matty-Patty's all grown up! Soon you'll be as tall as me!"

Mathilde giggled. Nana was almost as tall as Father, but that was another kind of lie grown-ups were allowed to tell. Mathilde didn't mind. Especially if it meant she was old enough to have a pony.

Nana's car smelled like grass and old books, but it didn't have a pony in it, of course. The rain made blurry lines down the windshield while the wipers went squeak-squeak back and forth. Mathilde drummed her heels against the floor of the car and tried to imagine the squeak was the sound of her saddle shifting as she rode her pony through the rain. She was so caught up in her thoughts that she almost didn't notice when Nana turned left instead of right at the corner with the big yellow restaurant.

"Where are we going?"

Nana smiled. "You didn't think I'd come all this way and not bring you a present, did you?"

Mathilde took a breath so big she felt like she might burst.

"But my birthday's not 'til tomorrow!"

"That's true." Nana gave her a great big wink. "But I won't tell if you won't. Besides, I think this is the sort of present you'd better pick out for yourself."

Mathilde could scarcely believe it. After all this time and all this waiting, she was finally going to get a pony of her very own.

Becky Hamilton was going to be so jealous.

But when the car stopped, it was in front of a store that didn't look like it had any ponies inside. The whole front of the store was covered in steel plates and the air smelled just a little bit like rotten eggs. It was very dark inside, but when Mathilde saw the rows of wire cages she knew she had been tricked.

"This isn't a pony store!" Mathilde said. "This is a demon store!"

Dozens of demons looked over at the sound of her voice. There were little, slithering ones and great big horned ones, almost as big as Mathilde. There were skinny ones with wings and spiky ones with eyes that flashed different colors. There was even one with brightly lit smoke seeping from the sides of its mouth as it chewed on something she couldn't quite see.

"Well, of course it is!" Nana said.

"But I don't want a demon!" How many times would she have to say it? "I want a pony!"

"Ah." Nana knelt down to put her hands on Mathilde's shoulders. "Demons make wonderful pets, you know. When I was a girl, we had a Belgian Muncher on the farm. They're smart as a whip if you train 'em right. Some can even talk. But do you know the best thing about demons?"

Mathilde shook her head, her lip quivering.

Nana leaned in very close and whispered in Mathilde's ear. "They're great for convincing parents that little girls are responsible enough to take care of a pony."

Mathilde didn't know what to make of this. Was it another grown-up lie? "Really?" Her voice trembled.

Nana smiled. "I've already spoken with your parents about it. If you prove you can take care of a demon…then maybe we can see about that pony."

Mathilde looked at the nearest cage. The demon inside was walking around on tiny cloven hooves and merrily cracking a little barbed whip. It grinned at her with a mouth full of teeth that gleamed like needles.

"Well, hello there!"

Mathilde jumped a little. Behind the counter was an old man with a checked shirt and large, round glasses. His face became a pile of wrinkles when he smiled. "Are you here for a new demon?"

"No," Mathilde said.

"Yes." Nana smiled. "It's her birthday."

"Oh." The old man gave that too-long nod that grown-ups gave when they thought they knew something but really didn't. "I see! Is this your first demon, miss?"

"…Yes." Mathilde looked at her shoes.

"Then this is a special occasion! What sort of demon were you looking for?"

Mathilde looked back at him. "I want the kind with the pretty eyes and the long, shiny mane!"

Nana sighed. "That's a pony, dear."

"Well, that's what I want!"

Nana gave Mathilde a sharp look, but the old man just laughed.

"Oh, I think I have just the one for you." He reached beneath the counter and pulled out a small glass cage.

The demon inside didn't have a long, shiny mane. It didn't have any hair at all, at least not that Mathilde could see. All she saw was a tiny, black, hooded robe that hovered above the bottom of its cage on a billowing cloud of inky blackness. Its eyes were two red stars that twinkled in the darkness of its hood like distant Christmas lights.

I guess that's kind of pretty, Mathilde thought.

Nana said, "Oh! What type of demon is that?"

"He's a Miniature Dark Lord," the old man said.

Nana clucked her tongue. "A Dark Lord? I thought they had great big horns!"

"Normally they do." The shopkeeper shook his head. "But this poor little guy was born without any. All the other Dark Lords rejected him. Even his own mother didn't want to take care of him! Can you imagine that?"

Mathilde could imagine it. She didn't want to take care of him either. But…"What's his name?"

The old man smiled behind his big round glasses. "Why don't you ask him yourself?"

Mathilde peered through the glass cage. She looked at the Dark Lord's tiny clawed fingers, at his dark billowing cloud.

Mathilde thought about her pony. "Hello," she said. "What's your name?"

"I AM IX'THOR, MASTER OF THE VENOMOUS PITS OF KARTHOOM!" The creature raised his arms over his head. He had a voice like the truck that picked up their garbage in the morning, only smaller. "BOW BEFORE YOUR MASTER, SMALL ONE!"

"How about that!" The old man raised his fuzzy white eyebrows. "He told you his name first thing! He must really like you."

"Well, I don't like him…" Mathilde crossed her arms. Ix'thor lowered his arms and hung his head a little. "…but I guess he'll do."

—

"IX'THOR…HUNGERS." The Dark Lord's voice rumbled from within its cardboard box.

"Dad!" Mathilde put her hands on her hips. "Hurry up! He's getting hungry!"

"I'm sure he's fine," Father said. He was kneeling on the floor of

Mathilde's bedroom, carefully hanging the curtains on the big glass cage. "You have to be firm with demons, you know. Give in and they'll walk all over you."

"IX'THOR DEMANDS SACRIFICE!"

"No!" Mathilde tapped her finger on the box. "Be good."

"All right." Father stood up and stretched his back with a soft pop, then turned down the light. "You can put him in now."

Mathilde placed the cardboard box in the cage and pried the lid off. Ix'thor wafted out, his black mist coiling around the bottom of his robe. He floated back and forth a few times, exploring his new cage.

"Here," Father said. "See the little altar down there? Put one of these on it." He handed her a small, softly glowing ball, about the size of a pea, from the big plastic bag Nana had bought. The bag said things like "Nutritionally Balanced" and "Now with extra innocence for a healthy glow!"

At the sight of the red pellet Ix'thor raced over to the altar and stood on top of it, his arms outstretched.

"Ah-ah-ah," Father said. "He has to take it from the altar. Make him wait for it."

"Shoo!" Mathilde waved her hand toward the demon. "Back up. Back up! He won't move!"

"Use the flashlight," Father said. Mathilde picked up the little light that came with the My First Demon book and shined it on the altar. Ix'thor went scurrying off into the shadow of his box.

Mathilde put the pellet on one of the divots in the flat stone and turned off the light. After a few seconds, Ix'thor came out of his box and drifted over to the altar. He leaned over, as if to peer at the pellet, then snatched it up with both hands.

"IX'THOR ACCEPTS YOUR SACRIFICE." The Dark Lord bowed his head over the pellet and devoured it. "NUM. NUM. NUM."

"Wow," Father said. "I guess he really was hungry."

Mathilde glared at him, her eyes wide and her cheeks puffed out. "See!"

Mathilde had a hard time sleeping that night. She was excited about her birthday party, but her thoughts kept drifting toward the pony she would have someday. What color would he be? What would she call him? She knew her pony would be gentle and tame, not pushy like Ix'thor.

How long would she have to take care of a stupid demon, anyway?

When she did fall asleep, she dreamed of ponies with glowing red eyes.

Mathilde woke up to something poking her in the chin. "Mnm." Mathilde swatted it away.

A moment later it happened again. She opened her eyes to see two red, twinkling stars and dark, clawed hands hovering over her face.

"KNEEL BEFORE YOUR MASTER, MORTAL!"

"Aaaaaah! Mom!"

Mother came to the door with Father and Nana close behind. When Mother flicked on the light there was a grinding squeal from Ix'thor, and the little Dark Lord scurried under her dresser.

"Turn that light off!" Nana said. "Or he'll never come out."

Father ran into the room and stumbled around in the sudden dark. "Where did he go?"

"How did he get out of his cage?" Mother asked.

"I see him!" Father lurched to the corner, but when he bent down, he banged his head on Mathilde's dresser. "Ow!"

Mathilde saw a black shape dart under the bed. She grabbed the little flashlight and crawled underneath the springs.

"He's right here!" She turned on the light.

Ix'thor tried to dart away from the beam, but he was trapped in the corner. When he hid himself in his robe, her hand darted out and wrapped around his leathery body. "I've got him!"

But she didn't have him. Tiny claws slashed at her hand, right between her finger and thumb.

"Eeeeeee!"

—

"I hate him!" Mathilde said through her tears. Mother wiped at her face, at the bubble of snot hanging from her nose. "I don't want a demon! I hate demons!"

"Oh, sweetie," Mother said. "It's just a tiny little cut. He was just scared of you, that's all."

"I don't care! I don't want a demon! I want a pony!"

Nana shook her head. "Sometimes ponies bite too, child."

Mathilde had had enough of this. "They do not!"

"Oh, you think so?" Nana said. "When I was a girl, my best friend Sheryl had her finger bitten clean off!"

Mathilde looked up through a blurry curtain of tears. She couldn't tell if Nana was making fun of her or not.

"You have to be careful with animals, Matty-Patty." Mother stroked Mathilde's hair. "Sometimes when they're scared they lash out. They don't know any better."

"But I was being careful!" Why didn't anyone believe her?

Mathilde looked up at the sound of Father's footsteps.

"Well that's that," Father said. "He's back in his cage. I don't know how he got out of there, but he'll need a cutting torch to do it again."

"I don't want him in my room!" Mathilde said. "I can't sleep when he's in there."

Nana sighed. "Maybe this wasn't such a good idea, Fred. I'm sorry. I'll take him back to the store tomorrow."

Mathilde suddenly felt queasy. Too late, she remembered her promise, her pony. "Wait!" Mathilde said. "I didn't…really mean it. He can stay."

Nana and Mother looked at each other. Nana looked like she was laughing at something, but Mother didn't look so amused.

"Do you really mean it?" Mother asked.

Mathilde nodded.

"Because this is your last chance," Mother went on. "If you say you don't want him one more time, we'll give him to someone who does."

"I know." Mathilde looked at her knees.

"You have to promise you'll take care of him, and be gentle with him."

"I promise," Mathilde said. "I'll take good care of him."

——

There was cake at the party. It was chocolate with white frosting and candy sprinkles, just like Mathilde wanted. And there were lots of presents, including a camera and a unicycle and eleven different kinds of toy pony.

Mathilde smiled when she opened each present, and because Mother was looking she made sure to say thank you to everyone who gave her something—even Aunt Maggie, who wasn't actually there. But she wasn't really happy. Even the unicycle, which she had asked for specially, didn't make her happy. When Robby Ferguson asked her if he could play with it, she said she didn't mind.

"This is so cool," Robby wobbled on the pedals, gripping the back of the couch. "I'm gonna get one for my birthday."

"I already have one," said Becky Hamilton. "It's okay. But I like riding horses better. Daddy says I can have one of my own for my next birthday."

"Yeah right," Suzy Feldstein said.

"It's true!" Becky tossed her hair in her stuck-up, Becky-Hamilton way. "I made him promise."

"I did get another present," Mathilde said. The other children all looked at her. "You want to see him?"

——

"You have to turn the lights down." Mathilde turned the dial down to a murky gloom. "He doesn't like light."

"What's in there?" Becky Hamilton stepped back. "It's not a snake, is it?"

"Sh!" Mathilde said, because she felt like it. "It's not a snake."

Mathilde opened the curtains around the cage and turned on the special red light in the lid, then stepped back.

The cage had changed since the last time she'd seen it. Ix'thor had moved around the pebbles at the bottom and stacked them up into a high-backed chair. He had taken apart his cardboard box and used it to build a little tower. Another piece of cardboard he had fashioned into a wide, diamond-shaped sword with tiny skulls carved into the blade. In the dim red light, it looked like every pebble in the cage had been worn down slightly to look like hundreds of itty-bitty multicolored skulls.

"WELCOME TO MY DOMAIN," Ix'thor said. "FOOLS. DID YOU THINK YOU COULD DEFEAT ME?"

"Wow!" Robby said. "That's cool!"

"What kind of demon is he?" Suzy asked.

"He's a Dark Lord." Mathilde felt the first stirrings of a real smile.

"No he's not," Becky said. "Dark Lords have horns."

Mathilde puffed up. "That shows what you know, Becky! This one was born without any horns."

"Does he do any tricks?" Robby leaned in to peer through the glass.

"Um…" Mathilde hesitated. "Not yet."

"BOW BEFORE ME!"

"You shouldn't actually bow," Mathilde said. "That just encourages him."

"Oh, man!" Robby was practically hopping up and down. "He's so awesome! I want a demon, too!"

"I can't have one," Suzy said. "My mom's allergic to demons."

Mathilde smiled at Suzy. "You can come over here and play with Ix'thor if you want."

"Really?"

"It's not that big a deal," Becky said. "It's just a demon. What good is a demon who doesn't even do anything? I bet he bites."

Mathilde's eyes widened and she pressed her lips together. Why did Becky have to be such a stuck-up brat? Why did Mother even invite her, anyway? Mathilde wanted to punch her, right in her turned-up nose.

"FOOLISH MORTALS," Ix'thor rumbled. "NOW BEHOLD MY

TRUE POWER!"

The inky clouds rolling around the bottom of Ix'thor's robe rolled up for a moment, as if being sucked back into his body. Then, his cardboard sword held over his head, Ix'thor emitted a burst of crimson fire from his hands. The eldritch flame danced along the edges of the blade, licking and curling, but not burning.

Robby looked like he was about to pee his pants. "Wow! You said he didn't do any tricks!"

"Well…" Mathilde tried not to look too smug. "Maybe he's got one or two."

———

It rained a lot in the fall. By the start of October it seemed like it had been raining forever. Mathilde slammed the door behind her and ran up the stairs to her room. She threw her soggy book bag on the floor and flopped facedown on the bed.

Her sobs mingled with the patter on the fog-painted window. In the darkness between the cage's curtains, two tiny red stars gleamed.

"WHAT TROUBLES YOU, MY MINION?"

"Shut up!" Mathilde said. "I'm not your minion!"

She lifted her face from the pillow and looked at the dark, wet imprint she'd left there. She wiped her nose.

"We had to make a collage," Mathilde mumbled. "About animals. And Billy Haggerty…he said mine was ugly…and he took it…and he threw it in the mud! It's ruined!"

"YOUR PLAN…WAS NEARLY COMPLETE?"

"Yes!" Mathilde squeezed her eyes shut. "Now I have to start all over!"

"DESTROY THE INTERLOPER!"

"Miss Hoevener says he's just being a boy. She said…that's what boys do when they like you. She says if I just ignore him then he'll stop."

Ix'thor looked down for a moment, then raised his sword over his head. "FEED HIM TO THE RAVENOUS TONGUE-BEASTS OF

GARAKH'NURR!"

Mathilde sniffed. "I would, but I don't know where that is."

Ix'thor reached out his little hand. "GIVE ME YOUR SOUL AND I WILL GRANT YOU LIMITLESS POWER."

Mathilde smiled a little. "Mom says I can't have limitless power until I'm older. But you can have a grub soul."

Ix'thor waited patiently by the altar, his eyes glowing brightly. "EXCELLENT."

—

On Halloween, a witch came to their house. She had a black pointy hat and a broomstick, green skin and a big, warty nose.

"Nana!" Mathilde ran forward for a hug.

"Oof!" Nana said. "This can't be my little Matty-Patty, can it? How's my little angel?"

"I'm not an angel." Mathilde raised the hood of her robe. "I'm a Dark Lord. Bow before me, mortals!"

"Oh, my! I think I felt the earth tremble there."

"Excellent. It is just as I have foretold." Mathilde looked up. "And Ix'thor's coming with us, too."

Nana looked outside. "Oh, sweetie, the sun's still out. I don't think that's such a good idea."

"It's okay. We got him a ball. See?"

Mathilde picked up the crystal ball, which was filled with swirling black clouds. From deep inside its murky depths, two crimson points of light could barely be seen.

"I made him an angel costume," Mathilde said. "But you can't really see it."

"SOON YOUR TRANSFORMATION WILL BE COMPLETE." Ix'thor's hollow voice rumbled from inside the ball.

Mathilde whispered, "I don't think he knows it's Halloween."

"Well then, let's not disappoint him," Nana said. "Shall we collect some souls?"

—

Orange leaves flew across the street in twisted whirlwinds while the shadows of barren trees stretched their fingers slowly away from the sun. Mathilde made her way down the street with Ix'thor's ball under one arm and her swollen bag of candy in the other.

"That's an awful lot of candy," Nana said. "I'm certain we didn't get that much candy when I was a girl."

"Ix'thor says fear keeps the peasants in line."

"Ah-ha. Mathilde…you know not everything Ix'thor says is a good idea, right?"

"Well, duh!" Mathilde rolled her eyes.

"Of course. How silly of me. Anyway, I think it's time we started heading back home."

"Wait!" Mathilde pulled on Nana's cloak. "Just one more street, please? Just to the end of the block?"

Nana sighed. "All right, but that's it. I don't want you crossing Washington Street. There's too much traffic."

"I won't."

"MWA HA HA," Ix'thor laughed with a rumble that made Mathilde's ears tickle on the inside. "NOTHING CAN STOP US NOW."

A cluster of trick-or-treaters was leaving the big stone house at the end of the street. Mathilde slowed down when she realized it was Becky and Sally Hamilton. She wanted to look away and cross the street, but Nana waved to them.

"Happy Halloween!" Nana said in her big, witchy voice. "Eee-hee-he-hee!"

"Hello." Mrs. Hamilton wasn't wearing a costume, just regular grown-up clothes and a bright orange vest. "Girls, say hello to your friend."

Becky and Sally were both dressed up in big, poofy dresses with lots of lace and glitter. Becky's was blue and came with a sparkling tiara, while Sally, who was a few years younger, wore a pale green one with fairy wings and a wand.

"Hello," Becky said. Sally just mumbled and hid behind her mother's leg.

"Hi." Mathilde noted with some satisfaction that Becky's bag had less candy than her own. "What are you dressed up as?"

"We're princesses!" Becky straightened her tiara. "What are you supposed to be? An ink stain?"

"Rebecca!" Mrs. Hamilton said. "That wasn't very nice."

Becky winced at her mother's words, but Mathilde just smiled.

"That's okay," Mathilde said. "I don't mind. I'll just take my revenge when I rule the world. Mwa ha ha."

For some reason grown-ups always thought that sort of thing was hilariously funny. Both Nana and Mrs. Hamilton laughed out loud. Becky just glared.

"Well, come on," Nana said. "We don't want your mother to worry about you. Nice seeing you, Kathy."

"Goodbye, Mrs. Clark. Say goodbye, girls."

"B-bye," Sally muttered.

"Bye," Becky said.

Mathilde started to walk away. She saw Becky's foot move, but didn't know what was happening until it was too late.

"Oops!" Becky said. Mathilde felt the edge of her robe yank, and then she was falling forward, her hands out in front of her. The sidewalk hit her knees, skinning them. Candy scattered everywhere, over pavement and grass.

Ix'thor went tumbling through the air, his ball reflecting the cold sunlight. It bounced once off the curb and once more off the side of a parked car. For one held breath Mathilde thought it was going to be okay, that the ball might roll harmlessly to a stop.

Then her hope vanished in the heavy squeal of brakes and the sound of shattering glass.

Mathilde screamed, trying to stand up, trying to run. Later she would remember Nana's hands grabbing her, pulling her back from the edge of Washington Street, but, at the time, all Mathilde could see was the tiny shadow on the side of the road, with its crumpled paper wings shining in the bright autumn sun.

"No!" Mathilde kicked and squirmed in Nana's grip. There was a crowd of people standing around now. A row of stopped cars backed up on either side of the street.

"Cover him up!" Mathilde screamed. She tore her own robe trying to get away. "He needs dark! He needs the dark!"

"Mathilde!" Nana shouted. Mathilde ran over to the little body and kneeled over it, trying to give him some shade.

"Ix'thor!" Mathilde sobbed. "Please!"

"NO!" The little Dark Lord reached one hand toward Mathilde's tears. "THIS…CANNOT…BE. I AM…IN…VINCIBLE…"

———

"But demons are pretty strong, right?" Father said. "You said they're almost impossible to kill."

"Dark Lords are weaker in direct sunlight." That was the old man from the demon store, with his checked shirt and big, round glasses. "Much weaker. I'm sorry. I did all I could."

Mathilde sat in the dark of her room. She wondered when they would realize she could hear them through the door.

She wondered if she'd be that stupid when she was a grown-up.

"I'll talk to her," Nana said. "It's my fault that this happened."

"No," Mother said. "I'll do it."

The door cracked open. It was the only light in the room.

"Matty?" Mother looked around. "Are you in there?"

"You can turn the light on," Mathilde said from her bed. "It doesn't matter anymore."

Mother closed the door behind her and turned up the lights just a little bit.

"His tower fell down," Mathilde said. "In his cage. I tried to prop it back up, but it just kept crumbling."

"Oh, sweetie!" Mother sat down on the bed and pulled Mathilde into her lap. Mathilde squeezed her eyes shut. All the tears she had left were hiding in her throat, making a lump.

"It wasn't your fault," Mother said. "There was nothing anyone could have done."

Mathilde thought of Becky, but if it made Mother feel better to think so, then she wasn't going to argue.

"If…" Mother trailed off and tried again. "Father and I were talking to Nana. When you're ready, if you still want one…"

"I don't want a pony," Mathilde said. "I want Ix'thor. But I can't have him back, can I?"

Mother looked like she was about to cry. "No. I'm sorry."

Mathilde snuggled into her mother's arms. Mother did cry then, a little. After a while, Mathilde looked up.

"Then…can I get a pony with glowing red eyes, and crush the skulls of my enemies beneath his flaming hooves?"

Mother laughed a little and kissed Mathilde's forehead. "We can find one with glowing eyes, if you want."

Mathilde sighed into her mother's embrace, listening to her heartbeat. "It's a start."

ABOUT AARON CORWIN

Aaron Corwin lives in southern California, where he works as an actor and voice actor. His debut novel, *Born to Shadow*, was published in 2022.

GEMINI

SOPHIE GREENWOOD

A LOOK AT THE YEAR AHEAD...

Congratulations, Gemini, you've made it through to another year—and what a year you've just waded through. As we begin a new cycle around the sun and Saturn begins its descent through the sector of your chart that rules closure and transformation, try to leave last year's loose ends behind. What the stars have in store for you this year requires focus and vulnerability.

Grief is arduous, unmoored, unending—after the months you've just waded through, you know that better than anyone—but try to reframe the heartache by holding space for the grief of others. Pay close attention to what your loved ones are telling you this year; they may be sending vital signals that you are missing.

JANUARY

Do you feel that?

Pluto is due to circle through Libra on the second and, although the snow is still falling outside, you will feel like a tree in spring: winter's end is in sight and it's finally time to let your flowers bloom. An exciting opportunity for growth and transformation will emerge as the new year begins and, with it, the realization that you must change your outdated ways of seeing the world. You must wear new lenses that will allow once overlooked nuances to reveal themselves to you.

Gifts will help mend neglected relationships as Jupiter enters Cancer in your fourth house; now is an ample opportunity to take your child out to relieve yourself of the guilt you have felt lately when looking at her round face and unbrushed hair. Now is the perfect time to realize you are all she has left now. Take her shopping, buy her whatever she sets her moonstruck eyes on. Hold her hand as you try to hurry past the bric-a-brac vendor in the market with a scar running over one eye that you try to not look directly into. Sigh as your child releases your damp hand and toddles over to a black oak-mounted mirror at the side of the vendor's stall. Roll your eyes when she gazes dreamily into her own milky reflection, clammy hands grasping either side of the intricately carved frame, and begs you to buy it for the empty wall in her bedroom. Don't make eye contact with the leering vendor as you hand over the money.

FEBRUARY

At the start of this month, Mercury is due to reverse into your domestic fourth house, bringing tension closer to home. Don't let any changes in your family's behavior be the source of unnecessary worry or upset. Remember that grief affects us all in wildly different ways: where you choose to stay home and slowly rot from within, your daughter may choose to open herself up and expand her social reach.

Having said that, do pay attention to the people your loved ones have chosen to allow access into their lives. The energy they bring, be that restorative or destructive, will undoubtedly affect the domestic balance you've been working so hard to restore.

The new year wants you to cultivate openness and vulnerability:

Saturn will be by your side, restoring some much-needed tolerance. Your daughter speaks often about a new friend, and you quietly wonder when she had time to meet someone new since her father's illness led to her being pulled out of school at the end of last year. Remember, though: an open mind equals an open heart.

MARCH

Your child's new, nameless friend will start to unsettle you this month: this in and of itself may be concerning as it is not in your easy-going nature to worry, dear Gemini. Ask, with all the kindness and benevolence a mother can give, to meet your daughter's friend. Try to contain your frustration when your daughter refuses to let you near him.

Jealousy is a tough and complex emotion with many false roots, and it can be difficult to accept that a loved one is no longer as dependent on you as they once were. Use this as an opportunity to evaluate why it angers you to see her lean on someone else's shoulder for a change.

Be wary of the mirror in your daughter's bedroom. Pay close attention to your peripheries when you are near it.

APRIL

It will now be getting increasingly difficult to ignore the overarching feeling of paranoia that has crept into your domestic fourth house. With Mercury once again entering its dreaded retrograde midway through the month, you have until the 15th to sort out any personal and home matters that may have recently become chaotic and confusing. Subtlety is key here, Gemini, though we all know that it isn't your forte.

Curiosity will be bound to get the better of you, and the questions you ask that began as minor, inconsequential attempts to grow closer to your loved ones will quickly expose themselves as the paranoid delusions that they are.

All the same, keep an eye out for those whose behavior has worsened lately. Challenge your daughter when she speaks to you with a sudden apathy and moroseness from behind the slick, steaming roast chicken in the centre of the dinner table on a Sunday evening. Question her when you peek through her bedroom door keyhole and see her talking to thin, empty air. Yell at her when you see orange flames writhing over haphazardly placed logs in the fireplace on the far side of her room and don't listen when she insists it wasn't her that lit it.

Don't be surprised when she pulls away from you further, Gemini. She knows you don't understand; she knows you never have.

MAY

Early on this month, the summer skies will bruise as energizing Mars slams the brakes for a two-month retrograde. It is likely that growing tensions will reach breaking point this month. Be prepared for some intense domestic combustion; this challenging cycle could bring unexpected outbursts, fights, and erratic behavior if you don't pull yourself together.

Watch your daughter closely. Begin to realize that not everyone—and certainly not every*thing*—has good intentions.

Despite your best efforts, your daughter will continue to garble on for hours to dead air in the dim light of her room. She talks as if she is responding to someone, she nods as if she understands what they tell her.

With the red-blooded planet off-course, it will be easy to self-combust when your daughter grows more recluse and aggressive as days go by. Watch that you don't come on too strong—surrender, dear Gemini, and listen to the heavens for once instead of forcing your agenda.

JUNE

Count the days as your daughter gets worse, pull strands—and then chunks—of hair from your head as the weeks pass and her hostility grows, tally the sleepless nights as you lie awake listening to her scream and babble in a language you don't understand. Some nights, you will hear another voice, low and coarse, seeping from your daughter's room. It will sound familiar in a way you will struggle to place, but don't be afraid of it. It may bring a necessary—though surprising—change into your life.

JULY

It will be easy to get lost in circular thinking and unrequited desires this month; what could have been this year, had you just made a few different choices? What should have happened that somehow didn't? What is going to happen that you so easily could have protected your family from?

Try to find a way to see things in a new light. Luckily for you, August is usually a perfect time of year for overdue realizations to come to light:

Your daughter is no longer here and there is something else in her place.

Her room smells of rot. She stalks you around the house. She no longer eats, so you will soon have stopped making food for her. When she speaks, which is not often and never to you anymore, it is the devil's voice that unfurls from her cracked lips. She watches you while you sleep, grinning with yellowed teeth.

You will think about calling a doctor, but you never do. There are no numbers for exorcists that you can find in the Yellow Pages. Besides, you will tell yourself, ghosts aren't real.

AUGUST

Poor, dear Gemini. The last month of summer will see Jupiter fall through your sixth, health-oriented house, although you may have felt this coming for a while now. Eclipse season will also begin alongside the planetary shift, both of which, unfortunately for you, means more curveballs are being pitched as we speak.

Wake up one night in the middle of the month to find your daughter collapsed and unresponsive on the kitchen linoleum, her eyes lolling into the back of her head. She groans, gutturally and without breath.

Call the hospital, drive frantically behind the ambulance's red-blue streaks blinking against the scattered rain and grey night sky. Watch with tears blurring your vision as your daughter is restrained against her will to a white bed arranged neatly underneath humming fluorescent lights. Wince as she screams, hot and piercing, louder than you have ever heard it before, and catch your breath as she finally loses consciousness.

This will be the first time you have seen your daughter asleep in months. Relish it. Hold her cool, limp hand. Pray.

SEPTEMBER

Pay attention to what surrounds you this month; many things will require you to adapt. Remember that only those who adapt will survive.

By the end of the month, you will have stopped visiting your daughter's still, languid, body altogether. You will tell yourself it's because you hate to see her like this, but, really, you can't stand the smell. No one else will seem to register it but, to you, it will be difficult to endure the overwhelming stench for more than a few minutes. When the smell starts to follow you home, you will not be able to recall when it started. Soon you will think it has been there your entire life.

Noises from the attic will wake you from an already broken sleep. You will be plagued with nightmares, some involving your daughter, some involving a horde of strange and vile creatures, most involving both. Don't look too hard at the deep, black scratches that will appear on the upstairs hallway walls between your bedroom and your daughter's.

The noises will gradually bleed from the attic and into the walls. You will begin to wake most mornings in your daughter's bed, though you will have no memory of going there.

Neptune, ruling planet of dreams and illusions, will make an appearance in your first house in the latter half of this month, and this may affect your grasp on your identity. It is likely that you will doubt yourself, your past actions, even your current reality. Try to stay grounded. Take heed of what is really here. The rest is unimportant.

The night that you are woken by your daughter's singing—a sound you have not heard in months now—drifting from her bedroom, open her door to find a dark figure standing in the mirror. The room itself will of course be empty, and the singing will have stopped. You will not recognize the figure. You will think you are dreaming.

Peer into the mirror as the Mirror Man peers into you. Reach out; touch the milky surface, frosted with a thin layer of dust. The figure will do the same. Lose consciousness as your fingers meet.

OCTOBER

We hate to break it to you, Gemini, but Mars is due to start its dreaded descent into your sixth house this month, whilst Neptune continues to spiral deeper through Libra. It might be challenging to keep a handle on things, and it is likely that you will see a decline in both your physical and mental health. Take it one step at a time: remember, you can't give more than you have.

You will likely have abandoned your bedroom and taken to sleeping only in your daughter's, where, it will feel to you, time runs at a different pace. Be prepared for flu-like headaches, sharp abdominal pains, and debilitating fever. You will stop eating. Somehow, you hardly get hungry. The few times you do, you will take an unexpected pleasure in the various creatures that wander out of the forgotten red-brick fireplace—unlit since June—on the far side of the room: spiders and other insects, the odd rat or squirrel. You will lose chunks of time—stolen, you will think, by the Mirror Man. He will watch you as you sleep. He will talk to you as you dream. Fear not, Gemini: you are sick, and the Mirror Man will heal you.

NOVEMBER

It is a sad and unfortunate fact of life that, while some people walk alongside us to the very end, most serve their purpose in our lives and eventually take their own path—often towards their grave. Allow things to unfold as they should; don't fight what is destined to be.

It may be hard to accept that your daughter, finally stiff and cold where she lays wrapped in bleached linen under the fluorescent tube lights of her hospital room, has given in. As the fog melts into the grey sheets of snow under the streetlights outside your house, trust that everything has its place. Trust that you will be shown the meaning of such heartache soon. Understand that your daughter was not strong enough for what is to come.

You will not visit your daughter's body; you will refuse to answer the phone calls that begin to pour in. They will cremate your daughter in a small, contained blaze and mail you the rubble afterwards. You will not cry. The Mirror Man will look upon you softly. He will whisper into you and tell you, finally, that his name is Avnas.

DECEMBER

Imagine yourself floating out to sea on a life raft or dinghy: if you try to swim against the tides, that will be exactly where you feel the most resistance, and that is where you will be most in danger.

The easiest thing to do is to surrender, fully and without apprehension, to the powers that have guided you this year. Allow them to fill the gaping space that has been emptied by your grief. The vulnerability you have cultivated this year will help; give into it, like a corpse, drowned by the river's current, being swept downstream.

Spend your days gazing into the mirror. You will lose all sense of time: begin to wonder why it even mattered to begin with. Avnas will thank you for the sacrifices you have made. All of it pays off this month, sweet Gemini: think of yourself as a snake shedding its skin; a moth free from its cocoon, transfigured and drawn to the flame.

No one understands that true transformation is slow but inexorable better than you—be sure to welcome it.

Avnas smiles upon you.

NEW YEAR'S DAY, 3:31 A.M., JANUARY 2024

Some are afraid of chaos, the undefined, the unknown: you are not among them. You are a master of the indeterminate because you know—after the year you've had—that surprising things can come from disarray.

Allow your eyes to adjust to the darkness last year brought. So much has been taken from you; you have suffered so much grief, so much misery. Trust that all things are aligned as they should be, trust that it is nearly your time to dance in the flames.

You will not remember how the fire started.

The picture of you and your daughter pumpkin-picking last Autumn, framed above the fireplace in your daughter's bedroom, will be the first to be swallowed by the blaze. You will watch the flames lick the marbled corners and melt the plexiglass protector, blackening the edges of the picture slowly and then all at once until your static, smiling faces are lost.

As the house that bears so many of your memories crumbles and blazes around you, you stand on the once-pink rug in the center of the room and stare into the mirror you bought almost a year ago. Your eyes, clouded and vapid, look like milky cataracts. Your face is gaunt. You are naked and your skin peels back in slivers, like potato slices in hot oil, uncovering the raw, red muscle and scored tissue underneath. You will smile, catching a semi-opaque glimpse of a face that isn't yours pasted over your own, like a double-exposed photo. The face smiles back at you.

ABOUT SOPHIE GREENWOOD

Sophie Greenwood is a non-binary writer and horror enthusiast from London, UK. She holds a degree in English Literature and Film Studies from the University of Southampton, where she wrote fervently about Trollhunter and Dead Snow. She is a Pisces.

WHERE IS DANIEL DESOTO?

ANDREW KOZMA

So there I was, throwing rocks at Daniel's window. Not pebbles. Rocks. The kind that star the glass with cracks if you don't get the fuck up and answer the window, Daniel. I picked up a rock with some heft, and knew I'd have to throw it at the siding of the townhome or it'd sail right through the glass and splash Daniel's room with brilliant shards. Daniel would understand—he's my boyfriend, after all—but his parents would scream and call the police. I just escaped juvie, so I can't chance it, even if the sound of broken glass is music to my ears. Some real John Cage shit, as my older sister would say.

My sister is *older*. By a decade. I was barely in grade school before she was out of our wonderful educational system entirely, going to college and dropping out before I'd even had my first period. My mom was pissed. She'd turned Offie's bedroom into her "creative refuge," filling it with craft tables for her scrapbooking, macrame shit, bottlecap windchimes, and whatever the fuck else caught her fancy. Then she had shove all her precious art into the attic where the mice and squirrels would gnaw it to pieces, all so my sister could move back in and *find* herself. Well, I found *her*. She's right in my fucking house, always whining and moping. Sometimes I think I ended up dating Daniel just so I'd have somewhere to go instead of sitting at home, listening to my sister complain that her "tragic" life is all Mom's fault for naming her Ophelia to begin with.

At least if she went and drowned herself in the bayou there'd be some beauty to her tragedy.

"You don't mean that, Sarah," Daniel would say, trying to make me into the nice, caring girl he thinks is hiding inside me, as if I'm a butterfly trapped in its cocoon.

I throw the rock—it hits the siding with a satisfactory thud, adding one more dent to those I've made over the past few months. But Daniel still doesn't rip his curtain back to mouth "Stop it," so I scour the ground for another rock. Right when I find one with edges sharp enough to embed the rock in the siding for good, a voice hisses at me from above.

"He's not here," his little sister says, her narrow face scrunched like she's sucking on sour candy.

"What are you doing in his room?" I ask. Daniel hates anyone being in his room if he's not there. Even me.

"He left to break you out of juvie." She pulls the window all the way open and straddles the sill like it's a pony. "Did it work?"

"No. I broke myself out. Where is he?"

Instead of answering, Allie slides off the sill and lets herself down the outside wall until she's hanging from her fingertips, then drops. It's then I notice she's fully dressed and I've never really paid attention to her the entire time I've known her. Although she's only a year younger than me, she's just been in the background, wearing boring clothes—high school camouflage—and never speaking up unless she's forced to.

Now she's wearing ripped black jeans and a black t-shirt, chunky black boots like knockoff Docs, and has a leather shoulder bag she's opening up to pull out a blood-red leather book I thought I'd seen the last of. The Desmocraton Codex.

"What are you doing with that?" I hiss.

"What are you angry about?" Allie says, her narrow face pointing towards me like a blade. "If anything, I should be the one who's angry!"

And she is angry. She keeps her voice down, because she's not an idiot, which I respect, but she is really fucking pissed.

"*This*." She hits the book hard with the flat of her hand. "Is what my brother wouldn't stop looking at ever since you'd been put away for your own good. He shut it whenever I walked in on him, but told me he'd found a way to help you."

I can't help frowning. "I don't need anyone's help."

"That's what I told him!"

A light flicks on in another room of the house. I can't afford to get caught, especially not by Daniel's parents. I've run away from juvie before, and if I'm caught they're going to throw me in for another six months. I'll miss the *entire* school year.

I pull Allie away by the hand, taking The Desmocraton Codex at the same time. I don't want to hold it. The cover feels like sweat-cooled skin. But it's not her responsibility, or her fault.

It wasn't Daniel's, either, so I don't know how it got in his hands. I'd covered the book in gasoline, set it on fire, and thrown its ashy remains in Buffalo Bayou; it definitely shouldn't be in my hands right now, its cover slightly greasy to the touch just as it was before I'd destroyed the fucking thing.

When we stop to huddle under some trees, the book's cover darkens in the dim light. It looks like an old scab.

"Where is he? Where *is* he?" I don't realize I'm shaking her until she breaks free of my grasp, stronger than she looks. "We need to find him, fast."

"What? You didn't answer any of Daniel's letters, and not a single phone call! And you expect me to believe you actually care now?"

"Where is Daniel?" I step back. "I'm not asking again."

Her eyes light up with bitterness and disdain. "Your money's still in his room, you know. He didn't touch a bit of it. It's under his bed, in a box labeled Birthday Shit."

"Why are you telling me this?"

"So you don't have to keep pretending you care."

She glances meaningfully at Daniel's open window and then walks off, snatching the book from my hands as she passes. The side of their house is old brick, and easy enough to climb if you know how. I'll never admit it to anyone—except maybe Daniel—but the reason I came back *was* to get that money. I need to leave town. I was going to try to convince Daniel to come with me, but if he didn't—his loss.

All I need to do is climb that wall and get the money and then I'm gone, home free. Free of home. And I think about it. I really do. It would be so easy. I could be on a bus to Austin or LA or Chicago in just a few hours and say goodbye to Houston forever.

But I wouldn't be able to live with myself. I couldn't write Daniel or answer his letters, because it hurt too much. The expression on his face as they took me out of the courtroom was so terrible, how he was trying to be comforting and positive and smiling because he didn't want me to be upset, but his eyes were empty, as if I was the abyss he was looking into. He was more devastated than I was, and somehow that's what I couldn't handle.

When I catch up to Allie, she looks at me with shock, her mouth a tight bow of distrust. We're in public now, away from the protected yards of those who want to pretend they suburb when, in fact, they urb, and an occasional car passes down Montrose side streets. I ask her once more where we're going, where Daniel is, but she doesn't respond. Fine, I won't ask again, even though the need to know burns in me. I don't like not being in control.

Offie took over being a second parent after Dad left and Mom decided she was done with everything about family life aside from the basics of keeping us clothed and fed. Even while she guided me through school, making sure I did my homework and advising me on how to handle those girls who'd decided I was the ugly duckling, I could tell she didn't want the responsibility. I hated not having power over my life, which made me angry at her for having that power and not wanting it. If I learned anything from all the counseling I was forced to go to over the years, it's that part of the joy I got from making trouble was making Offie's life hell. And I could be in control of being punished, owning all that I brought upon myself.

But right now, I'm not in control. And based on Daniel having the book, he's not, either. He doesn't know what he's dealing with.

"Fuck your savior complex," I mutter under my breath.

"Talk about my brother like that again, and I'll punch you in the mouth." Allie says it casually, and I don't doubt she will. I'm not afraid of her, but still, I respect it.

"Let me have the book."

She hugs the Codex to her chest, already possessive of it.

"Not until you tell me what's going on. What's Daniel's savior complex got him into this time?"

"I can't tell you what's going on until I have the book."

"Then I guess I'll live in ignorance."

Again, she walks off as if she doesn't care if I'm following. I know she *does* care—she thinks I have some special knowledge that'll help Daniel, but I'm also positive she'll go on by herself into whatever danger there is regardless. She's stubborn in the exact way Daniel is not. He let me do whatever I want, convinced he could persuade me to curb my worst impulses when I was already in the midst of them. He's an idealist.

Allie is pragmatic. It's obvious she didn't know Daniel was gone until she'd heard the rocks I was throwing. Her bag jangles like she'd shoveled every possible thing she might need inside it, from lip balm to a flashlight to the kitchen knife she keeps in her room for late night cheese snacks no one else needs to know about.

It's late. Only a few cars haunt Westheimer. A racer zooms by, engine roar a dragon in the night. In the silence after, there's a freight train whistle miles away, though it sounds so clear it could be coming from the next block over. Electronic music bleeds through the upstairs window of a fourplex as a night heron stalks the gutter for frogs. When I was a kid, I collected those frogs in a jar in order to feed the next night heron I saw and forgot about it, as kids do, and all those frogs died for no reason, except to freak my mom out the next time she searched through the garage.

I'm not a good person. Daniel is. Allie might be.

"The book is used for summoning…things."

I tell her this as we cross West Alabama Street. I know we're headed towards Menil Park, that giant expanse of ground which used to be an apartment complex where, for several generations, people lived, fucked, suffered, and died. It's better than a graveyard for summoning—at least that's what I told Daniel once when I was sad and drunk off scotch I'd stolen from my mom.

"Summoning demons?" Allie asks, as if we're talking about a new place to buy clothes.

"No. Sure. I guess." I look away from Allie's curious gaze. "I don't know what to call them, but they're dangerous."

"And Daniel…?" She lets the words trail off, fear and disbelief in her voice.

"I might've told him that the book can fulfill your wildest dreams."

"Can it?"

I pause. My heart thuds into my throat. "Yes."

The tall oaks of Menil Park rise up over the houses surrounding it, their shadows blacking out the ground. Menil Museum security patrols the place at night, but they mostly just sit in their cars and watch shows on their phones. It's a quiet neighborhood.

Then we hear the screaming. It's like the sound of one animal dying in the jaws of another, or metal girders bending under the stress of hurricane winds. I'm running before I even know what I'm running toward. The park is bordered by Richmond Avenue, a tall wooden privacy fence, and museum buildings, all dark. Across Richmond is a dead strip mall, most of its storefronts abandoned shells. There's no one else to help us if we need it.

Under a clump of trees near the fence, I see the faint glow of a dying fire. A number of figures dance through the glow, their movements stuttering like video on shitty wifi.

"Daniel!" Allie screams. She's faster than me, sprinting off through the park until she's just another of the shadows against that glow. And she still has the Desmocraton Codex.

It isn't a book I found in a library. It's not a book I heard about online. It's a book that was born, as far as I can tell, from my mind. My hopes. My desires. It's why Offie hates me and I can't stand her, even if *she* doesn't know why.

With Dad gone and Offie at school, I spent my nights praying for a different life. It wasn't really prayer. I don't believe in God, or gods, or a higher power, but I was convinced, out of desperation, that something out there could change my life, because if it couldn't, and didn't, then I'd die. For two weeks straight, I reached out to whatever might hear me and pried apart my innermost thoughts seeing if there was something inside me I could release. A needful hunger burned in every single cell of my body. Sometimes, on the edge of sleep, I closed my eyes and felt myself inside myself, a smaller body in my body, and a smaller body inside of that, down and down until I finally reached a tiny me buried in those hundred other mes, my skin rough and dead and needing to be shed.

One morning I woke up and the book was on my bedside table. I didn't have to touch it to feel the depth of its promise, that if I opened its covers and just read a few words, my life would be livable again. Whatever I wanted would be mine.

I wanted my parents to be who they were when I was young. Or if not my parents, because my dad was often a shit and my mom didn't really care about anyone but herself, then someone who cared about me. I opened the book.

Within a few days, Offie had returned to Houston to live in her old room, having found college overwhelming, depression all-consuming, and the resulting loneliness unbearable. And she cared about me, but she cared too much. She wanted to live her life over again through mine, and I couldn't stand how she'd martyr herself at her job waiting tables or take Mom's cutting sarcasm about her being a failure because she knew it would free me from being a target.

Her return seemed natural. I thought it hadn't really been my wishing that brought Offie home but her own failure, as my mom never stopped pointing out. So laying in bed a few weeks later, I succumbed to my own self-hatred. I opened the book, fulfilled a small ritual from its pages, and wished I had the same number of friends as everyone else at school. An electric burn traveled from the book up my arm to the center of my chest and settled there.

The next day a sickness spread through school, a fifth of the student population coming down with a never-before-seen variation of mono. The once overcrowded buildings became a ghost town.

The book had power.

And I used it. To get revenge on the girl who reported my smoking to the principal. For stupid stuff, like money for a new tattoo. And for the pettiest purposes, like silencing the all-night music from the restaurant next door that kept me awake at night.

Every single thing I wished for came true but made the world worse than before. With each wish and ritual, the book grew thicker with more densely-written pages and disturbing illustrations that seemed to twist on the page, until I opened it one day to read words in faded ink that addressed me directly.

dream me more

That's when I burned the Codex and threw its remains into the bayou. I watched it float on the scummy, trash-spotted water. I stayed there until it sunk under, all at once, as if nabbed by an alligator.

From then on, my life was my own again. Every prank I pulled, every adult I disobeyed, every small thing I stole from the corner store was mine and mine alone. Whatever consequences I suffered I would've earned. Every burst of pride I felt at having not been caught, that was mine, too.

Daniel never wanted to own up to anything. That was his whole reason for not getting in trouble in the first place, even if he never admitted it to himself. The book would eat him up in one swift bite.

"Sarah!"

Daniel calls my name, but I can tell by the tone that he's not yelling at me.

When I reach the edge of the trees I find one of the illustrations from the book made real. A line of burnt grass forming a perfect summoning circle. A few smaller protective circles grow like warts along the edge, each large enough for just one person to stand in. A cluster of candles burns in the center of each circle—tea lights that barely give off any light and burn for no time at all, but are cheap enough that a high school student could afford hundreds of them. Three dead grackles lay inside the large circle, equidistant from each other to form the points of a triangle.

Daniel stands in one of the protective circles, Allie a few feet away from him as though she's afraid to touch him. They both stare at a third person on the other side of the circle.

It's me.

Another me, trapped for now in one of the protective circles.

Allie turns back to look at me—the real me—then to the other me. I take a step toward her and she yells, "Stay away from us!" and rushes to Daniel. She gives him the Codex. All of the light in the small copse of trees bends towards the book like steam caught in the flow of someone's breath.

Daniel, oh Daniel. I haven't seen him in weeks, and I thought maybe I'd idealized his looks in my imagination, but the reality is so much sharper. He's wearing that old gray hoodie that's full of holes and the tan jeans he has to wash every time he wears them because they attract dirt like a lint roller. There's a crookedness to his nose, a constellation of tiny moles on his right cheek, and his right shoulder hunches up just a tiny bit higher than the left. All of this I'd forgotten.

As the light draws towards the Codex, it burns away those imperfections, smooths out his skin, straightens his posture, makes him the most perfect version of himself. The me that faces him across the summoning circle is the most perfect version of me, too, as if airbrushed by social media filters, tightening this, exaggerating that, my eyes too large and too dark, a smile inviting you to everything you ever wanted to do but didn't dare. Inviting Daniel. He can't look away. Even Allie screaming right next to him doesn't break his focus.

"Daniel!" I yell, my voice breaking whatever hold the other me has on him.

She turns her attention to me. I expect her expression to shift to anger or hatred, but I see only hunger reflected in my too-perfect eyes. She takes a step towards me but jerks to a halt. She can't cross the protective circle's border. Whatever is happening, I'm not a part of it yet.

And I clearly shouldn't be.

The Desmocraton Codex was born from me. Or I brought it into this world from somewhere else. Everything in it, everything that it does, is tied to me. Standing this close to the circles in the grass, to the book, to Daniel, to the other me, I can feel the lines connecting all of them. I'm not *part* of those lines, but I could be if I tried. I don't know what that would mean. Just like coming here to help Daniel instead of grabbing the money from his room and leaving, there's no going back if I make myself part of the pattern.

I could still go. Even without that money.

But Daniel is looking at me now, really looking at me, in a way that he's never looked at me before. Is the Daniel I'm seeing now the Daniel I've always known, or has the book already shifted him into someone new? Or am I the one who's different? Our eyes lock and a jolt passes from him into me, my chest tight, my throat dry, every muscle tense like I'm on the edge of a cliff. I want to bury my face in his chest and let the musty smell of his hoodie block out everything else.

His eyes slide away toward the other me. And why not? She's perfect, even if she's not me. Daniel holds the Codex in front of him and slowly raises it towards the sky. The pattern he's drawn on the ground feels like it's been sewn to my nerves, and it's tightening, as if one final tug will bring it to completion.

Allie tries to reach Daniel, but the circle keeps her out. Her eyes dance between me and that other me, hate and fear turning her gaze to broken glass.

"Get him away from here," I yell at her, then step over the circle of burned grass.

Instantly, the other me runs over the broken circle and barrels into me before I can brace myself. I don't *feel* anything, like she's a ghost, but I find myself on my back anyway. The book is in my outstretched hand, the leather cover ragged like skin scraped raw. My cheek rests on the trampled, burnt grass, the ashy smell filling my nose. Allie drags Daniel toward home, both of them already turned away from me and the remains of what Daniel tried to do.

Red-and-white lights flash at the edge of my vision as I lie there. I've saved Daniel. Menil security will find me. I'll go back to juvie. I don't think I'll ever see Daniel or Allie again.

I don't know what Daniel was trying to do, but I feel *her* inside of me. That other me. My body is a dress yet to be fitted and my tongue explores someone else's mouth.

"Dream me more," my voice says.

My left hand reaches up and closes my eyes.

ABOUT ANDREW KOZMA

Andrew Kozma's fiction has been published in *Escape Pod*, *Daily Science Fiction*, *Antipodean SF*, and *Analog*. His book of poems, *City of Regret* (Zone 3 Press, 2007), won the Zone 3 First Book Award, and his second poetry book, *Orphanotrophia*, was published in 2021 by Cobalt Press. Check out his Patreon at https://www.patreon.com/thedrellum.

TO DUST

CASSIE E. BROWN

Steel-shell black, ruptured concrete gray: the ivory dust that settles from a mortar shell. The dark eyes and winter wheat-colored hair of Illinois farmboys who are fed rations of lies and GMO corn. The war catching, jumping on the wind like sparks on a vast plain of the endless Kansas prairie. Midwest heartland, hot and smoldering. *Who are they?* Tracer fire in a night sky burning an unnatural green: lighting up the fears of the world from the nuclear winter in the false spring of carbon-warming. Azure blue skies offer no cover, gleaming through broken roadside Catholic church windows under shattered, concrete crosses. Glass still casting colors on the floor from minerals mined from mountains and lakes: cerulean blues, veridian greens, and a red the color of the wounds of their anointed, weeping Christ. Fainting in church pews and the apoplectic faces ringing endtimes bells. *Who are they?* Industrialists transform chicken farms with tin roofs overnight with wartime urgency—chemical spills into creeks burn eyes, acrid—brown pools reflecting laser fire. Railroad tracks spill rust the shade of dried blood onto barn floors as welders' sparks fly like sunshowers onto sizzling water-pools; post-capitalist metal transformed into curlicues of spikes to slow the advance of the rollers. *Who are they?* Rumbling shakes Cedar Rapids streets where people once carried steaming coffees—fragrant, earthy steam rising. Instead billowing now from the ground is bitter, dry dirt the deep charcoal of a tired Earth— breath of a nation beneath sidewalks now gasping under their weight. *Who were we?*

ABOUT CASSIE E. BROWN

Cassie E. Brown (she/her) is a writer of long and short form fiction, poetry, and essays. Her work draws inspiration from her childhood in rural Missouri, classic children's literature, and her experiences as a queer misfit. Cassie's work explores what is ugly, beautiful, and true about rural places and fairy tales. Apart from writing, she is a clinical social worker and a tea aficionado. Find more at www.ozarkmisfit.com.

GRAMS

NICHOLAS JAY

After they processed her, I packed what was left of Grams in a box. She'd been stuffed with seeds and peat and wrapped tightly into a pill-shaped duffel of bark-brown biodegradable mesh, somehow no longer than my forearm and no wider than my head. One word, "AfterGrow®," was emblazoned on the bag in bold, turquoise letters. For a moment I pictured her in there, desiccated and compressed. Her mouth open, full of dirt. I shivered and shook my head, jostling the image loose like an Etch-a-Sketch.

The cardboard box I packed her in made for a crude coffin, but it's what I had. I covered her duffel with soil and set her on the windowsill so she'd get plenty of sun. After a few days the first shoots sprouted, little tendrils of nascent green pushing up through the soil.

When I signed up, the AfterGrow customer service rep ("Grief Support Agents," they called themselves) said tending to Grams would be easy, that they only implanted hardy varietals that thrived in a wide range of environments and could survive people with clumsy green thumbs. And if I struggled at all with caring for her, the hotline was always open.

Easy or not, I took care to water the plants every day. Couldn't let Grams die all over again. Far more challenging would be keeping her here at all, perched on the windowsill like a gargoyle. Sometimes, if I stared at the box for long enough, it appeared to swell and ebb. Taking breaths, drinking in the air and the sun. Part of me yearned for that illusion, but a stronger part of me rejected it.

My sister, Naomi, found the whole concept of AfterGrow cruel. Not for Grams, but for her survivors. She couldn't stand to look at Grams when she came over. But our jobs waiting tables didn't leave us money for a burial, and I couldn't stand the thought of cremating her. Fire stripping away her essence, wiping the slate clean. Naomi had a fondness for clean slates. Scorched earth. No respect for the time it took to grow something. To nourish it.

"Fire *is* nourishing, Asher," she argued. "Just ask the pine trees."

"Not so nourishing in a crematorium," I scoffed.

The first flower to bud was a lily, Grams's favorite. It had an oblong, pink-and-white bulb framed by thick outer leaves raised up like prayer hands. After that came a freckled vine with large leaves striped green and purple. The leaves bore the same violet shade as the long, flowing caftan Grams wore for special occasions, the one with the gold filigree. And their green hue matched the jade earrings she favored. I'd never seen a vine like that. So peculiar, in an exciting and disquieting way, how evocative it was of her essence.

I sent a picture to Naomi to see if she knew what it was. She replied with a link to an app that identifies plants from pictures. "Go to town, Ash," she wrote. A signal to leave her out of this.

In no time at all, Grams was covered in plants of all types. More lilies had sprouted, and several more shoots of the purple-striped vine snaked around the other stalks. Periwinkle, phlox, and other creeper flowers hid beneath broad leaves from other vines. Pothos, maybe. Each leaf bore unique patterns, squiggly and chaotic tangles of sage-green lines meandering through the leaves' waxy, emerald-green remainder.

I uploaded new photos to the app, but they all came back unidentifiable. I called the AfterGrow hotline to ask about them.

"The seeds we use are proprietary," explained the Grief Support Agent. "That's why your app won't recognize them."

"The patterns are so cool. You should document them!"

"They are marvelous, aren't they?" she said. Her laugh was buoyant, stirring. "Unfortunately for science, client confidentiality takes precedence."

Over the next several weeks, I settled into an unremarkable routine. I watered Grams every morning around ten—earlier if I was working brunch that day—and measured her soil moisture when I got home, checking as gingerly as I could for root rot. In between, my shifts passed in a blur of cramped kitchen hallways and hot oil and "Behind!" and forced smiles and the warm, herbal smoke from an offered joint or cigarette.

Taking care of Grams was an antidote of peace and quiet. The initial excitement of seeing her first sprouts had worn off, now that it was harder to measure her growth. No casual gardener or plant-parent I knew had ever mentioned anything about the comfortable mundanity of completing the same tasks, day in and day out, to keep something alive. I began to understand the impulse to accumulate more plants, to have more to take care of.

But I didn't give in to that impulse. I wanted to do right by Grams, and she was enough for an amateur. Her vines grew and grew, drawing strength from the soil and the remnants of her bones. They grew so long, their weight threatened to drag her off the windowsill. I put up some dowel rods in the window and guided the vines up and over my makeshift trellis.

My apartment became as humid as a greenhouse. As the plants flourished, they filled the air with sweet, cloying perfumes of flowers and wet wood. Every so often, I'd catch a whiff of sharp mint, like the Listerine strips Grams devoured like candy before she got sick. I kept the window open most nights to freshen the place. Spring had turned to summer, so it was warm enough now.

Grams always preferred the warmth when she was alive. Every afternoon, she'd settle into her favorite rocking chair like a mama bird roosting in a tree. Back when Grams and Naomi were still speaking, we would spend hours on the front porch together. Naomi and I would play checkers on the floor while the three of us invented stories about Grams's eccentric neighbors. As Grams got sicker and angrier, Naomi couldn't bear to spend much time with her anymore. I would sit with her alone, watching the sunset, trying to make conversation when she was in a good mood, staying quiet when she wasn't. Eventually her in-home nurses helped carry that burden, keeping vigil on the porch when I wasn't around.

In death, Grams favored warmth too. Her vine-arms crept steadily toward the threshold, soaking up the sun, only she'd traded a rocking chair on her porch for a box on a windowsill. I'd come home from work and lean next to her, smoking a joint, sometimes two, gazing out at the pine trees' crowns swaying in the courtyard. I rarely made it home in time for sunset, but I was glad Grams could enjoy it from her perch.

By the end of summer, her leaves were bigger than my fist. Their variegated patterns had also shifted, transforming from chaos into cursive. When I watered her in the mornings, I'd catch glimpses of what I thought were letters decorating her leaves.

I convinced myself my mind was playing tricks on me until a new purple vine sprouted. At its tip were two leaves, each bearing a clear, elegantly-drawn letter. "A" and "N." Asher and Naomi, emerging from the same stem.

I immediately sent a pic to Naomi. For once she wasn't dismissive, sending back a short but sweet "Aww." I wiped a tear from my eye and celebrated the small victory.

From then on, every new leaf Grams grew bore a letter. More A's and N's but also plenty of others. Then she started sending them in two-letter pairs. The chaotic clouds of variegated lines grew longer and longer until they disentangled into full words. One near the base of the purple-striped vine read "sun." A pothos leaf read "peace." The leaves adorned with "A" and "N" now spelled my full name and Naomi's, too. On days when I'd wake up too early, unable to get back to sleep, I'd sit by the windows and study each one, holding them up to the soft dawn light and tracing their creases like a palm reader.

I sent more photos to Naomi, choosing words that evoked nice memories of Grams. "Tuck" for when she'd put us to bed, "game" for our front porch checkers matches, "swim" for the swimming lessons she gave us at the community pool. I left out "drown" from the same vine. No need to burden Naomi with the less happy words.

Her reply was short. "Bad juju," then a grimacing emoji.

"It's nice," I retorted. "She's bringing me joy for a change."

"It'll turn."

As Grams continued to grow, rising up and up to almost completely cover my windows, the words transformed again. "Sun" became "sin." "Game" became "blame." Over time, more and more of her nice words contorted into ugly ones. Some were references to her illness ("cough," "fluid"), while others alluded to death ("ending," "killing"). The leaves changed as well. They grew larger every day, but their edges began to wither and brown spots stained their middles like cigarette burns.

Before another tiresome brunch shift, I found seven leaves scattered on the floor below the windowsill, their stems brittle toothpicks. Each leaf had a different word on it, yellow cursive snaking through decayed brown. I shifted them around a bit, until the message clicked:

still a deadbeat as always, i see

Alarm, tingly and fast, skittered down my spine. I looked around my apartment, as though there would be anyone else who could confirm what I saw. Grams' box loomed above me, the bottom corners crusted with mold, the sides bulging from the extra biomass that sun and water and my own breath had nourished. Eyeless, she stared at me through the layers of soil and greenery. Ever vigilant.

I called in sick to work, then called the AfterGrow hotline. Maybe something had gone wrong with the seeds. Or with Grams. I held the leaves, crumpled in my hand, while I recounted their words to the Grief Support Agent. His voice was firm and measured. "It's uncommon, but with the right level of care, your loved one can send messages through the growth."

"What kind of messages?"

"Any kind, really. Depends on the person, their temperament, how much they left unresolved before they passed. Most of the time they're just shapes or letters or fragments of words. It's pretty rare to get some-thing so lucid."

I shivered. I thought of Naomi and her appetite for fire. Clean slates.

"Is there any way to stop it?"

"It's part of the natural process of unburdening," he droned, like he'd read this script a thousand times before. "Releasing the extra weight."

"So, no?"

"All of this should've been in your orientation literature. I can't shape the process. I can only help you through it."

"Well, great. Really helpful."

I hung up. Tried to swallow but couldn't. My mouth was as dry as dirt.

Maybe Naomi had been right. Maybe I hadn't researched After-Grow thoroughly enough. But Grams was here now, somewhere between alive and not-alive. I couldn't just abandon her.

"Yes, you can," hissed Naomi, when I called and said the same to her. "You don't need to let her control you anymore."

"But she's speaking to me!"

"She's *dead*, Asher. Whatever is happening has more to do with you than her." She sighed. "Look, you know what I'd do. Just torch the bitch."

I growled and chucked my phone across the room. I couldn't believe Naomi would be so disrespectful, especially because part of me believed she was right. This could all be over, and quickly.

I took deep breaths, matching the rhythm of Grams's box swelling and shrinking. My anger abated. The smoke in my head cleared. Embers of something, a product of some emotional debt I harbored, smoldered softly deep down in my gut. This would be a slow burn, not a bonfire.

Taking care of Grams was the right thing to do. If she had things to get off her chest, I'd hear them. All part of the process, even if it ached.

Tending to Grams had become second nature, but I was beginning to worry that her vines looked worse for wear. I gave her extra water before evening shifts to armor her against the harsh late-afternoon sunlight, but every time I came home, I'd find more leaves on the floor. I bought a plastic tub for her after roots burrowed through the corners of the cardboard box. Not much of an upgrade, but more structurally sound at least. The pothos and purple vines were the only plants left now, having choked out the lilies and creeper flowers. They grew ever longer, grasping at the sun and leaving behind long stretches of barren stem.

New messages dropped about once per week. Some I couldn't quite make sense of (*drain fluid from behind eyes, doctors and their blade fingers*), but some really hurt.

stuck in your ways.

never made time to visit.

always a lazy brat.

Things she'd said during those last visits. Things her *mouth* had said. Empty words, divorced from her mind, which was clearly elsewhere. Still, the words clung to me, wrapped around my bones like ivy on a trellis.

Every time a message dropped, I put the words in order, then took a picture before crumpling the leaves. For some reason, storing a memory in pixels was easier than holding onto Grams's physical remnants. More distance, or something. I made a note to call the hotline about that, but then deleted it. They hadn't done a great job of "helping me through it," or whatever the last guy had said.

After our last exchange, Naomi disengaged completely. I texted her often, alluding to Grams's messages, probing for sisterly advice, but she either missed the hints or didn't care. Or maybe she had nothing new to say. I could hear her smug, nasally voice in my head. "You should've read everything more carefully. You've only got yourself to blame. Don't come crying to me."

When winter arrived, Grams's vines dropped nearly all their leaves. The apartment became a swamp, air spongy and rank with decay. Mildew grew in corners among the cobwebs and along baseboards. As much as I wanted to ventilate the place, I kept Grams's window closed, buffering her from the cold as much as I could. If she had a fighting chance, I'd help her along.

I purchased a grow lamp and a portable rotary fan and hung both above her, but they didn't seem to help. Grams's vine-arms chattered like teeth in the manufactured breeze, losing more leaves and sending messages nearly every day.

cant hold on.

dont let me die alone again.

do something.

for once do something.

Every time I looked, it seemed more leaves littered the ground. Then an entire shoot from the purple vine snapped off and flailed across the hardwood floor.

do something.

do something asher.

do something damn it.

My hands trembled. Sobs pushed up from my stomach in heaves. I couldn't handle it anymore.

I called the hotline. "Help! She's—Grams is dying," I stammered, struggling to hold the phone. "I—I don't know what to do. What do I do?"

"It's okay," said the Grief Support Agent, her voice melodic and unfathomably calm. "Everything is going to be alright."

"The plants, I couldn't—I couldn't keep them—they're all withered, dying. Dead, actually. Dead as dirt." The fan sheared more leaves off Grams's vines. "And I bought this stupid fan thinking she needed air, and this grow lamp thinking she needed sun and—" I marched over to the windows and ripped their power cords out of the wall. "They did jack shit."

"Deep breaths, Asher. I want you to take deep breaths. In. Now out."

I did as she instructed, but the rush of air did nothing to untangle the knot in my stomach or quench the smoldering embers of my guilt.

"That's good," she continued. "Keep breathing like that, slow and steady. Now, tell me more about the plants. How do they look?"

"Brown. Leaves are brittle. Vines are weak and drooping, like I said. What should I do? How do I fix this?"

She laughed softly, the way someone laughs when they've solved a riddle. "There's no need to fix anything. This is natural. The plants are dying because they're running out of organic material."

"So we need more. How can I get more?"

"It's a *good* thing, Asher. It means your Grams is becoming unburdened. Finally."

do something. asher. cold. hurt. why wont you do something.

"Time to let go." Her voice was soft but firm. Urgent.

I dropped my phone and crossed the room to the box. For a moment, I contemplated reaching into the dirt, feeling through the roots and rot to touch her, to see how much was left. How much time she had. Maybe I could add to her, shore up her reserves. Stick my head beneath the soil and suffocate. Fill my mouth with dirt. Let the plants eat away at my hair and skin, worm through my ears to my brain and unburden me, too.

I looked out the window at the trees in the courtyard. Naomi's voice rang in my head.

Fire is nourishing. Just ask the pine trees.

I opened the window. The cold air wafted into the apartment, pushing out the humid cloud Grams had created. It stoked the slow-burning fire in my gut. Making it grow. Making it rise.

Grams's leaves shivered in the wind. Some snapped off.

no no help do something so cold do something damn it

Carefully, I unthreaded her vines from the dowel rods and laid them in a pile on top of her. I grabbed her bin and took it downstairs to the courtyard, setting it a short distance from my favorite pine. A tall, gangly thing swaying aimlessly in the cloudy, winter sky.

I reached into my pocket, took out my lighter and a joint. I lit it, drinking in the herbal smoke. Warmth flooded me.

I cradled the shriveled stalks of the purple vine and the pothos, braiding and unbraiding them between my fingers. Holding Grams's hands in mine for the last time.

Then I brought both of the vines to my lighter's little flame. It lapped at the stalks, eager to drink.

Once the fire caught, it raced down Grams's arms like a swarm of ants. The flames consumed everything, now dry as chaff. The vines, the leaves, Grams's last words. All gone, milled to ash. I took one more drag and exhaled, my smoke swirling and dancing with hers.

ABOUT NICHOLAS JAY

Nicholas Jay is a conservation-minded urban planner living in Atlanta, Georgia. He enjoys his time most with either pen, violin, or map in hand—sometimes all three at once. Find him on Twitter at @kn1ck-kn4cks.

INSECTIVORE

ANDREW KOZMA

Murtha Snattleby decided she was going to eat bugs, and that was that.

She started with what she found under her bed, a solitary spider surrounded by a few lonely mummified gnats. It didn't back off as she set out her tongue as an onramp, but stepped up instead, its legs tickling as it walked further and further in. As she swallowed the spider, Murtha imagined it setting up shop in her stomach, a web stretched across the width of it to catch what falls in. A warmth spread out from the center of her body. She was pretty sure it wasn't spider poison, but spider good-feelings, the arachnid finally belonging somewhere.

Murtha Snattleby sampled ants next. She'd heard they were a delicacy. People ate them drowned in chocolate. They tasted like Rice Krispies. The front yard was dotted with dirt cones like infant volcanoes, each disgorging streams of black ants. She knocked a hole in one nest to rile the ants, and in a few seconds they covered the damage like a bandage. They swarmed over her hand, and she stuffed it into her mouth, licking every tiny black-pepper morsel until her hand was clean again. The ants were poppy seeds with legs, miniature kernels squirming between her gums and her cheeks, exploding with a snap between her teeth.

A cicada was harder to get. Murtha sampled the husk left behind on trees, an unsalted potato chip. And she snuck out of her house at night to catch an emerging cicada as it dug itself out from its self-imposed exile and tossed the dirt-covered bug into her open mouth like a kernel of popcorn. But what she really wanted was the harsh buzz of the adult cicada, its car-alarm cry rattling through her teeth, her skull, her entire skeleton.

But adult cicadas hid in the high tops of trees. And if Murtha got too close to a cicada, it shut up right quick, its scream silenced like a computer shorted out by a lightning storm. When she stepped away, the cicada would start again, letting her hear the smarminess in its song. *You can't catch me! You can't see me! You can't find me! Ha! Ha! Ha!*

Most people would have given up at this point and turned to easier fare. Lovebugs, for example, who hitched together at their hind parts and unconcernedly waltzed into your open mouth. Or Junebugs, those clumsy fliers, who always seemed to be discovering just where they are, startled antennae nervously aflutter. Murtha Snattleby was a Snattleby, however, and Snattlebys never admit defeat.

She climbed every tree on the block, scouring every limb for the cigar-stub shaped cicadas. She stole the cigar stubs from her father's study and created cicada decoys with her pens and her paintbrush, with paperclip legs and tinfoil wings, and set them around her house, hoping to lead the real cicadas into making new friends. She mimicked the cicada's raucous rattle, so perfectly she even fooled her parents into thinking a cicada had broken into their house, though the effort left her voice scratchy and cracked like one of her mom's treasured vinyl records.

None of her plans worked.

In fact, when she finally found a cicada to eat, she almost missed it. Murtha was walking home from school, her mind occupied with what a scorpion would taste like, and whether it would make friends with the spider in her stomach or they would fight, and, if they fought, would she feel it, and would it feel like a stomachache or like a massage?

And while her whole being was engrossed in imagining this, she almost stepped on the cicada, only stopping because right before her shoe came down on the insect, it rattled, it buzzed, it screamed as only a cicada (and now Murtha) can. She barely kept from crushing it, freezing at the exact moment the sole of her shoe rested on the hard cicada head, and its wings blurred so much they looked like the plastic wrap Murtha's dad used to wrap her lunch sandwiches.

Murtha pulled back, but the cicada didn't fly away even though its wings hummed for a few seconds longer. It took a wobbly few steps towards the edge of the sidewalk like a cheap mechanical toy. She knelt down close to it, putting her lips inches away from where she imagined the ears were.

"Don't worry, Mr. Cicada, it won't hurt much at all."

She picked up the cicada quickly and didn't let go when its wings went into overtime. She expected that it would scream at her, that its piercing siren buzz would emerge as a last-ditch effort to free itself. But it didn't do that. Its wings stopped. It turned its head towards Murtha's face. It wanted to know, she knew, what kind of creature was about to eat it. She could see her reflection in its glossy, pea-sized eyes.

She tossed it into her mouth and smashed her teeth together, eager for the texture and the taste of the bug.

But the cicada wasn't there. She could feel it deeper in her mouth, its legs dancing on her tongue as it moved towards her throat. Before she could spit it out, it climbed down, and she couldn't feel it anymore. Her mouth felt dusty, but other than that, the cicada could never have existed at all.

That night, her stomach rumbled and vibrated. It burbled and sang. Her bones shivered and her skin tingled the way Pop Rocks felt on her tongue. When she opened her mouth, the cicada's scream came out. Her bedroom window rattled with swarming cicadas, eager to find the way in.

ABOUT ANDREW KOZMA

Andrew Kozma's fiction has been published in *Escape Pod*, *Daily Science Fiction*, *Antipodean SF*, and *Analog*. His book of poems, *City of Regret* (Zone 3 Press, 2007), won the Zone 3 First Book Award, and his second poetry book, *Orphanotrophia*, was published in 2021 by Cobalt Press. Check out his Patreon at https://www.patreon.com/thedrellum.

MERLOT

JORDAN HIRSCH

I slip my needle in the
wine, ABV not strong enough
to kill anything but my
nerves.

Pulling her closer, some parts
are still useful. Some parts are
still good. How much I can take?
Simple

averages, really. A bit
here, a bit there, leaving just
enough so that she remains
her,

and I — I travel back to
a past that promised more than

pain. A moment when monsters
hid

only under beds. Each pass
of needle catches, a chip
in its bone shaft tugs as I
sew

myself complete, stealing from
the girl I once was. She's done
nothing wrong but survive. She's
done

nothing wrong. Neither did I.
I offer her a sip, too,
numbing before I remove
more

past to graft onto myself.
I am no monster.

ABOUT JORDAN HIRSCH

Jordan Hirsch reads, writes, and dreams about space in Saint Paul, MN, where she lives with her husband and cats. You can find links to her published works on this site and find her most current book reviews in *Whistling Shade* literary journal. She's a member of SFPA and served as the Elgin Award Chair in 2021 and 2022. Jordan recently received her MFA in Creative Writing with an emphasis in Fiction from Concordia University in Saint Paul and is a first reader with *Flash Point SF*.

PICK A DOOR

B. GARDEN

Shannon paces before the two airlocks at the far end of the capsule, waiting for the little lights above the door frames to shift from flashing red to solid green. Mechanical hissing and grinding escalates from the other side, the same way it has for the last hundred or so rooms, vibrating the metal flooring and tickling Shannon's toes in her prison-issue boots. She pictures the new pods shuffling about like some sort of macabre shell game.

The lights turn green. Shannon's brain stutters, her stomach rolls. She can't make herself choose.

"Refusing to pick a door is not in your best interest," says the voice of the Jailer, piped into the room through invisible speakers. "It will only add unnecessary time to your sentence. Please pick a door."

The words come in the polite, almost cheerful default voice of the Aggrecore, the AI mindnet that governs the space station. It almost sounds like it's grinning at her. Shannon's irritated, anxious brain latches onto it.

"Change voice settings," she says.

"Inmates do not have customization privileges," it says. "Please pick a door."

"Fuck you."

Her gut is telling her that something is different this time. Maybe there was an extra second of hydraulic hissing, or a variation in the vibrations. She tries to go back through the sequence in her memory, closing her eyes to focus.

"Please pick a door," says the Jailer.

"Just—god dammit," she says, waving her hands wildly. "Give me a minute."

She scans the doors, trying to find some visible difference. Both are matte gray, peppered with rivets, and reinforced with symmetrical bands of metal. She tries to count the rivets, but she loses track of the numbers over and over again. She peers at the metal plating from various angles, looking for warping, condensation, any hint that either of them is holding back the vacuum of space.

"There is no difference in the doors," says the Jailer, "Please pick a door."

"I said give me a minute," Shannon says, the words hissing through her clenched teeth.

"You must continue passing through doors. Please pick a door."

"Yeah, but if I pick the wrong one, it will launch me into *space*," Shannon says, her voice escalating into a shout. "So give me a fucking minute!"

The words echo briefly in the metal-walled pod before they disappear. In the station apartment she shared with her husband, their yelling had vibrated in the cheap light fixtures and flimsy cabinets. He would occasionally augment this by slamming a fist into the wall, adding a certain punctuation to their frequent fighting. Once, it had been enough to knock the last piece of his great-grandmother's china, which the woman had smuggled aboard the station in the first wave of residents, off its decorative little shelf in their dinette. Of course, that had somehow only been Shannon's fault.

"There is a chance that the door you pick will lead to your death," says the Jailer. "Please pick a door."

"Fine. Fuck," she says, her voice hoarse now. "Left."

Shannon shuts her eyes, holds her breath. Every muscle and tendon that can tense, does.

The door opens.

No rush of air, no forceful ejection, no yawning, star-flecked void. Just another room.

Shannon releases her breath, and then feels something different release from somewhere inside her gut.

She races inside, gagging, frantically scanning the pod. There's a toilet in the corner, lid open. She rushes over and vomits the remains of her dinner into the open bowl as the door whispers closed behind her.

Shannon catches her breath while the room vibrates and the new capsules are put into place on the other side of the two new doors. She wipes the edges of her mouth with a square of toilet paper.

"Your vitals indicated a high probability of emesis."

"What?" asks Shannon.

"Vomiting."

"Oh."

"We have prepared you a snack."

Shannon takes a second to examine the rest of the pod.

"Ah. Must be bedtime," she says, realizing at that moment how badly she needs to lie down.

Tucked against the wall, there's the same bed as always, with the same mattress, the same scratchy blanket and the same change of clothes, but there's a new addition this time: a small bedside table with a tall cup of water and a sandwich on a plate. The sandwich is cut into triangles, with alternating ribbons of soybutter and imitation fruit jelly glistening between layers of soft white bread.

Shannon briefly pictures a little serving drone rearranging the room, preparing and cutting the sandwich for her. It's the most thoughtful thing someone has done for her in a very long time.

"Wow," says Shannon. "Thanks for the sandwich."

"You need sustenance to continue passing through the doors," says the Jailer.

"I take it back. Fuck you," says Shannon, grabbing the sandwich and waving it in the air. "This better not be artificial grape flavored."

"Your preferences are in our database."

She relishes in the sandwich, takes a long sip of water, uses the toilet, and then climbs into bed.

"Can you at least tell me," says Shannon as she burrows under the covers, pulling the blanket as tight around her as possible, "if the other door, that last one, would have led to my death?"

"There's a chance that the door you pick will lead to your death."

The lights turn off.

It takes Shannon a long time to fall asleep.

—

Within four hours of killing her husband, Shannon had been arrested by security drones. The hearing had taken place in a small, faux-wood paneled room.

Shannon sat alone and picked at the brownish flakes of drying blood around her fingernails while several distinct Aggrecore voices updated her on the proceedings. The trial opened with pious oration about mathematical functions of chance and closed with her being sentenced to Justice Probability 3-6422A.

Her Aggrecore-partition lawyer informed her that it had successfully argued for this Justice Probability, even though the Aggrecore-partition prosecutor had initially sought Justice Probability 2-6413C.

"And is that better?" she asked numbly.

"Significantly."

"Thank you."

"You're welcome."

"Do you have anything to say on the matter?" asked the Aggrecore-partition Judge.

"It was sort of self defense, if that wasn't clear."

"Your Justice Probability reflects this."

"Okay. Good. Thanks."

As the strangely cheery drone guided her from the judiciary wing to the penitentiary wing, saying things like "almost there," and "if you have any questions, please don't hesitate to ask," Shannon had plenty of time to speculate about what people were saying about her. What they would say if she never came back.

Most people in the sprawling, city-sized space station thought of the airlocks as something that happened to strangers, or friends of friends. Tales of both survival and ejection were whispered in bars and coffee houses. Shannon's late husband had survived the ordeal three times before he met a more certain fate involving her kitchen shears. Each time he came back, she had to digest the conflicting swirls of relief and resentment that warred in her stomach. She would wrap her arms around him and whisper, "I knew you'd come home." And he would smile and say, "Yep, charges were bullshit. As always," even as the evidence lingered in Shannon's fading bruises.

———

Shannon is yanked from sleep by a single, percussive clang, ringing in the wall right next to her head. She grips the blanket like a lifeline.

"What the hell?" she says. Adrenaline wipes aside any grogginess.

Silence, save for the beating of her heart. She briefly pictures a frozen corpse crashing against the metal shell of the station, breaking into a thousand small pieces.

"What was that?" she asks.

"Please disregard." The Jailer's voice makes Shannon jump. "That was not a part of your sentence. We apologize for the inconvenience."

Shannon sits up and reaches for the glass of water. Her hand trembles, sloshing a bit over the rim. "You can make it up to me with a Valium."

The Jailer does not respond.

"Okay then. Lights, please," she says.

"There may be many doors before the next bed," says the Jailer.

"Well, check my vitals. No way I'm falling back asleep."

The lights flick on. The bulbs above the two airlocks are solid green.

"Please pick a door."

Shannon gets to her feet and rubs her arms in an attempt to calm the trembling. She changes into the fresh set of clothes, then stands in front of the two airlocks.

"Right door, please."

Shannon closes her eyes, holds her breath, braces for death. The airlock disengages. The door opens.

Another room.

Shannon exhales and imagines how her late husband must have felt facing each door, picturing him standing at each precipice, tapping his foot, his face smug in the same way it had been when she had first grabbed the kitchen shears.

"Oh, what are you going to do, stab me?" he had asked, laughing.

Her respiration accelerates out of her control. The wiry muscles in her neck yank on the back of her head, constricting her scalp until it feels like her skull will burst. Through the thumping of her heartbeat in her ears, she can hear the Jailer say something about holding her breath and counting to four. Shannon hunches over and tries to catch her breath, throwing a middle finger up for the Jailer.

After a few moments, she manages to lay on the floor and sprawl her limbs out. The cool, metal floor underneath her is comforting.

Mechanical noises come and go, the pod vibrates. The ceiling seems to sway above her as her hyperventilation subsides. She hates the color. It's the same prefab sheet metal as her apartment ceiling, with the same bleak gray finish.

"I think I need to see a doctor," said Shannon.

"You do not need a doctor. Please pick a door."

"You're not a doctor."

"Your vitals are acceptable."

"Why do I feel like I'm dying?"

"You experienced a panic attack."

Shannon sighs. "Can the next room have a couch, or a shower

please?"

"Inmates do not have customization privileges," says the Jailer, "and you were warned that there may be many doors before the next bed."

"Fuck you."

"Please pick a door."

"I don't want to die!" Shannon yells, slamming her hands and feet against the floor like a child having a tantrum.

"There is a chance that the door you pick will lead to your death," says the Jailer.

"I know," whimpers Shannon.

"Please pick a door."

Every muscle in Shannon's body cramps at the thought of having to choose another door. She starts to cry. The tears well in her eyes slowly at first. But they accelerate, and before long, Shannon is weeping, her body spasming with the agony of utter, helpless fear.

She sputters on the floor for some time after the storm passes inside of her. Snot and tears slick her cheeks, but she doesn't care.

Then she takes a deep breath, and the breath comes easy. She hazards a smile. The muscles of her mouth move effortlessly.

"Okay," she says, rising to her feet.

"Please pick a door."

"Left."

Shannon keeps her eyes open this time. The airlock disengages. The door opens. Shannon does not die.

She strolls into the new pod, her muscles limber and loose, but the smile melts from her face.

The room has only one door, the light above it already green.

Shannon waits for the vibrations, for the mechanical cacophony. But there's only silence.

"Wait… what is this?"

"Please proceed through the door."

"But, there's only one."

"Yes, this is your final door."

A shout builds in her stomach, but it loses pressure before it can erupt from her throat.

"Already?" she asks. Her voice sounds so small.

"Your sentence will be complete when you pass through this door."

"What's behind it?"

The Jailer does not respond.

Little twitches bubble in Shannon's muscles, impulses to fight, to flail, to punch the walls, to turn and throw herself against the closed door behind her, but there's nowhere to run, nobody to fight.

Well, almost nobody.

"You're a bastard," she says, looking up into a corner of the ceiling where she imagines the Jailer watches from. She's surprised to find that the words come out with a chuckle.

"Your feedback has been logged," says the Jailer.

Shannon sighs and takes a step. Her body refuses to fall into the rhythm of walking. Her subconscious won't take over. She has to will the muscles to move. Each step is an active decision, every inch is deliberate.

Finally, she slumps her forehead against the door's cool, uncaring metal.

"Alright," she says, "I'm ready."

The door opens.

ABOUT B. GARDEN

B. Garden is a bartender, baker, and aspiring ghost. They recently challenged God to a chili cook off, but have yet to hear back. You can rifle through their belongings at www.godcompost.com.

DREAMBLASTIC™ STIMULATING WHITE NOISE BOOST YOUR PRODUCTIVITY LUCID DREAMS NIGHT LIGHT ROTATING LAMP -

★★★★★

HAZELLE LERUM

Before, my dreams were useless,
like dreaming of chopping too much cabbage,
        or that you never died.

Sometimes I dreamt of rubbing against a large balloon and it felt like sex.
Other times I dreamt of sex and it felt like rubbing against a large balloon.

I still dream of my teeth falling out, but now instead of dry-swallowing,
I dream of mouthguards   to tame their roaming geology,
whitening strips   to strip their history,
and veneers   to fix their shamefulness outright.

Like before, I dream of my exes: *HBO, Netflix, Paramount+.*
I dream of flying: *American Airlines.*
And I dream of showing up to school pantsless: *Victoria's Secret.*

I no longer dream about your death,
or having to explain gender to my parents,
or all my long-dead pets in a cold sweaty ball.

Instead I dream of cream spread over thin limbs.
I dream of dildos shaped like krazy-straws, and sheets silky as a
bud.
I dream of myself, fragrant with purpose.
I dream I bump into the woman who picked my coffee beans at the
park,
and she is dressed colorful and she is happy,
                                        happy,
                                        happy.

Now when your heart stops as it often does in my worst nightmares, the
iPhone 14
dials fast and sweet, and the operator knows the exact words to start
your heart again.

When our Toyota Camry plunges over the cliff face, we float to the
surface
like beads of cream, smiling and giggling like gulls.

ABOUT HAZELLE LERUM

Hazelle Lerum (@hazellerachelle) is a Portland-born writer who works
full-time in the COVID-19 pandemic response. Her poetry has
appeared in *Waterwheel Review*, *HORNS*, is featured in the Mochila
Chat podcast, and has been anthologized in the national anthology of
best undergraduate writing, *plain china*. This poem is the product of the
Clarion West Flash Fiction Workshop 2022.

UNDER PRESSURE

R. L. MEZA

At the bottom of the Mariana Trench, Death is a misplaced pinprick, a hairline crack. Owen hears Death tapping at the exterior, testing the structural integrity of the habitat. Irregular ticking echoes through the lab, as if the light deprivation has thrown an invisible clock off-kilter, altering the nature of time itself. Days pass in a blink. A second stretches to eternity while Owen listens to Death searching, hunting for a way in.

A loud creak makes Owen jump. The beaker of solvent slips from his fingers to shatter on the floor, and for an instant he can feel the frigid water coursing through the broken porthole. He can taste the salt. Before 16,000 PSI can crumple the habitat like a tin can, Nora looks up from her data analysis and says, "Would you relax? You're putting me on edge."

The habitat has no portholes. Embarrassed, Owen cleans up the broken glass. He moves to the freezer to collect another specimen, to restart the extraction process. *Discodermia nox*—a new species of sea sponge—has lured Owen 11,034 meters underwater. It produces a specialized form of discodermolide, far more effective at combating cancer than *Discodermia dissoluta*. Owen hates the sponge for bringing him here, but he hates himself more for not discovering it sooner, years before he met his wife. Before Cassandra's cells turned traitor and Death came to claim her.

"*Owen*," Nora says. Her tone makes Dylan's head whip up; the sealed containers of harvested discodermolide rattle as he sets the storage cube aside. "You're making a mess. Take the night off—*rest*. And eat something, for Chrissake. You're skin and bones."

Owen shuffles from the lab without argument, down the short tube to the living quarters, bypassing the galley. He's not hungry or tired. He paces as much as his cramped compartment will allow: three steps to the bunk squashed against the bulkhead, three steps back to the thick steel hatch. When he finally sits on the bed to remove his shoes, a trickle of fine sand forms a tiny pile on the floor. Owen frowns into his left shoe. He kneels to inspect the pile.

The particles are soft, flesh-toned.

His right shoe is empty. Owen peels off his socks. He brushes his left heel and stares at the dusting of particles coating his palm in alarm. He sweeps the pale sand onto a square of paper and folds it, setting the sample aside for a time when the lab is vacant.

All the while, Death ticks and taps.

Groaning.

Begging to come inside.

—

As Owen suspected, the particles are not sand. He peers through a microscope at the miniscule clusters of human cells—not flakes, but misshapen granules. Elsewhere in the habitat, Nora and Dylan are engaged in a game of cards. A burst of laughter straightens Owen's spine. He backs away from the microscope, puzzled.

Because he can still feel the paper against his skin, the folded square containing the sample from his shoe. A meter of space stands between him and the slide on the microscope's stage, yet the cold press of glass generates a full-body chill. The gooseflesh stippling his arms appears flatted. A headache throbs in his skull. Wincing, Owen gropes his nose to be sure the cartilage is still standing erect. The ache in his head intensifies.

Owen removes the slide and lifts the cover. The pressure in his skull vanishes. As he scrapes the stained smear into the paper packet, a fine trail of cells pours from his sleeve onto the counter.

He doesn't know why he ignites the Bunsen burner, doesn't understand the force compelling him to pinch the fleshy sand between his fingers and sprinkle the granules into the flame, when every instinct is screaming at him to conserve the crumbling cells. He's never self-harmed before, too afraid of the pain. But since *she* died, not a day has passed without the temptation presenting itself in a thousand different—

Owen chokes. It is not the sensation of self-immolation that sucks the air from his lungs, but the realization that he cannot recall the name of the woman he loves. The physical agony hits a half-second later. He barely feels it, combing trenches through his memory in search of…

He breathes a sigh of relief through gritted teeth. The name is gone, but her face remains: bright eyes, like pools of liquid amber; round cheeks; thin lips, prone to part in a mischievous grin; a narrow gap between her two front teeth. *Her, her.* Her name is…

A flower, maybe.

Owen adds the remaining sand to the paper packet. He longs to seal the cells in a plastic bag but fears he'll suffocate. The persistent chill prickling his skin necessitates a careful sweep of the counter and floor, to locate the errant cells, but the search only scatters more of Owen around.

A name from mythology. Roman? No…

Owen removes a bag of rubber bands from a drawer. He dons a pair of gloves, then winds the bands tight around the cuffs of his blue jump-suit, wrists and ankles. He'll worry about his head later. Footsteps are approaching. Nora enters the lab, yawning.

"Tell me you haven't been in here all night," she says. While Nora sips her coffee, pulling a face at the bitter swill, Owen slips the paper packet into his pocket and nudges the Bunsen burner back into place with his elbow. "No," he says, "just got here a few minutes ago."

Morning already? Owen shivers from the lingering chill. Somewhere in the lab, he's still drifting freely.

A knock sounds, ringing off the habitat's shell.

One, two. Three-four-five. Six.

Coffee sloshes over the rim of Nora's cup. She curses. Owen says, "You heard that?"

Nora scowls up at the metal dome shielding them from the weight of the Pacific Ocean. "Detritus, probably."

The knock comes again.

One, two. Three-four-five. Six. Followed by an insistent clicking. Owen pictures his wife's manicured nails drumming the outside of his office door, preceding her entrance with the meal he missed, lost in his work. Too engrossed in the depths to treasure—god*damn*it, *what is her name?*

"Owen? You okay?" His wife cocks her head, listening.

Again, the knock sounds. Owen blinks and Nora is back. "It's probably nothing. I wouldn't worry," she says.

"Awfully deliberate sounding, for nothing."

Nora nods, slowly. "Mm-hm. Sounds like a piece of equipment came loose. Dylan, go check the control room."

Dylan stops short in the doorway and grunts his consent, grumbling as he switches directions. He returns from the control room and says, "Nothing I can see from in here. Comms and sensors are all functioning."

Nora's scowl deepens. "Hull integrity?"

"One hundo. I could send a divebot out..." Dylan tilts his head, mimicking Nora and Owen. "I don't hear—"

The knocking rings through the lab.

"Huh," Dylan says. "Almost sounds like the secret code my brother and I—" A shadow clouds his face. "Never mind. Can we just ignore it?"

Owen cringes. Nora catches the twitch and her expression softens.

She says, "I won't be able to concentrate if that keeps up. It's already driving me crazy." She glances at her watch, lips counting off the seconds in silence. "There it is again. Every thirty-nine seconds."

"What the hell?" Dylan glances at Owen, cowering in the corner. "What's up with you? You look like you've seen a ghost."

Owen's toes are squirming in his shoes. Curling fine sand into tiny piles.

"Fine," Dylan huffs, "I'll send the divebot out. But you're covering my station, Nora. I'm not getting docked for wasting time on this."

"I'll go with you," Owen says. "I'd like to watch, if that's okay?"

Dylan raises an eyebrow at the rubber bands cinching Owen's cuffs, then jerks his chin at the door, as if to say: *Whatever, man. Let's get this over with.*

While Dylan is busy prepping the machine, Owen dips a hand into his pocket. He smears a dusting of cells across the divebot's skin.

Dylan and Owen evacuate. The launch begins.

Owen watches, tense, as the chamber floods. The exterior aperture spins open, releasing the divebot into the abyss.

It feels like drowning.

Like freedom.

Owen collapses.

———

He regains consciousness in the medbay, a compartment just large enough to accommodate the horizontal medpod aligned against one wall. Nora turns sideways as she enters, stooping to avoid bumping her head. No space is wasted in the habitat. She taps the medpod's console, checks Owen's vitals. When she notices he's awake, she says, "How long has it been since you last ate?"

Owen tries to shrug the question off, but the restraints hold him secure against the gel cushion. He's exposed, stripped down to his yellowed underwear. Nora doesn't ask when he last showered—not that the absorbent powder they dry-scrub over their skin resembles anything close to hot water. If he used either method to bathe now, he'd likely disintegrate. The exfoliation of the powder would sand his grainy flesh down to the bone, while the pressurized spray of a shower would wash him away entirely, like waves crashing over a sandcastle. Owen's eyes pop wide. He answers Nora with a question of his own: "Where's my jumpsuit?"

"I comm-linked with the surface," Nora says. Her short dark hair is a riot of frizzy tufts, standing on end, as if she's been yanking on it. She won't make eye contact. "They're sending a shuttle down at the end of the week to retrieve the bulk of the frozen sponges, along with the discodermolide we've extracted."

She pauses. And then: "Owen, they're pulling us off the project…automating the hab. Dylan and I will stay on for a few weeks, to help facilitate the switch. But once the new tech is in place, we're out on our asses. They're bringing down more divebots to harvest the sponges. They plan to use the hab for storage. An AI-guided shuttle will transfer the stock to the surface for factory extraction. Big pharma's drooling over—"

"Why now? What changed?" Owen sees Nora flinch. "What did you tell them?"

He can feel Nora's pulse quicken. Did she touch him without gloves on? Owen's mind is detached, numb. He can't stop shivering.

"You're hypothermic," Nora says. "Dehydrated, anemic. You haven't been taking care of yourself."

"Don't change the subject. What did you tell them, Nora? Was it about the dive, the knocking?" Owen listens, but he can't hear anything over the beeping of the vitals monitor. "What did you see, Nora?"

"My—" Nora coughs. She scrubs her mouth with the back of her wrist, rubs the purplish suitcases under her eyes. And it's as though her mind has reset, replacing her haunted expression with one of morose determination. "Nothing, Owen. There's nothing out there. Look, I didn't want to do this here, but…they told me about your psych eval. They know you fudged the results somehow. You have no business being down here, not so soon, after Cassandra—"

"Who?"

Nora's eyes narrow. "Your wife?"

Owen searches through memories set adrift, like the cells he released into the abyss. He touches the image of a woman with sunlight in her hair, white lace cascading over her curves. The sound of her laughter is excruciating. His mind recoils, seeking the cathartic sensory deprivation of the ocean. But his cells are drifting far from the habitat, farther from each other. The effect is fading, leaving only the pain.

Another memory surfaces: a woman hollowed out, cored, like a once-shiny apple riddled with worms. Her eyes are dull, her lips cracked. She screams as if her lungs are filled with broken glass.

Thirty-nine seconds he waited, after the screaming finally ceased.

Thirty-nine seconds before he gathered the nerve to enter her bedroom, despite the urging of the hospice nurse.

But she was already gone. *Cass...*

Owen's hands clench into fists. Her name is escaping him. His fingers are bony sticks, divesting particles like dandelion seeds onto the gel cushion. Soon, there will be nothing left of him.

"My wife is dead," Owen says. It's the first time he's spoken the words aloud. Another Owen completed the mandatory psych eval, an identical shell—the same version of himself responsible for paying the kid next door to hack the mainframe and tweak the results. The same shell that rode the shuttle underwater, away from a world he was no longer fit to inhabit.

But now the shell is decaying, revealing the quivering meat within.

"You said you and Dylan are staying on," Owen says. "What about me?"

"You'll be leaving with the shuttle. I'm sorry, Owen." Nora pats his fist. She wipes her hand on her jumpsuit after. Owen wonders if she's aware of the cleansing gesture, or if the motion is subconscious. "It'll be good for you."

"But it's my discovery—my project. You can't just throw me away."

"*Our* project," Nora says. And Owen thinks, *Ah ha. Here it is—the excuse she's been waiting for.* "It's not up to me, Owen. They never would've let you come down here, if they knew."

"But if it *were* up to you? You'd have the project all to yourself— you and Dylan. All the funding and the credit, yours."

Nora looks at Owen as if he's slapped her. "They're getting rid of *all of us*, Owen. You'll get your credit, but the rest is for the machines." Her gaze shifts to the bulkhead. "We were never meant to stay here. It's not healthy, being this isolated."

The next morning, Nora releases Owen from the medpod. She confiscates his keycard, revoking his lab access, but spares him the indignity of locking him in his quarters. Owen's free to wander the confines of the habitat. He peppers every crack and corner with the cells showering off his bones, until he feels more like the structure holding back the ocean than the pathetic creature trapped inside. His jumpsuit hangs in baggy folds. He paces, restless.

Death clicks outside, ticking and tapping, matching his stride. Snatching up the deflated cells floating beyond the habitat and devouring them, one by one. Memories blink out in Owen's mind, like dying stars.

The resulting void is intoxicating.

When Dylan and Nora turn in for the night, Owen creeps into the control room to access the footage from the dive.

—

A spotlight crawls over the convex shell of the habitat. Particles swirl in the beam. As the light advances, a fluttering shadow retreats, trailing stringy tendrils over the curved horizon.

The divebot crests the apex of the habitat and descends into perpetual night. The spotlight probes the darkness. Bubbles of liquid sulfur and carbon dioxide rise from nearby vents in the ocean floor. Bioluminescent comb jellies flicker in the distance.

The camera jiggles, as if struck from the side. The divebot's propellers whir, attempting to correct course, to dislodge the anchoring force dragging it down, away from the habitat. The camera rotates. Skeletal appendages blur at the periphery, then leap into focus.

A bulbous mass fills the frame.

Teeth like pins. Glinting amber eyes.

Owen jerks back from the screen, uttering a breathless cry. He replays the video from start to finish, seven times. Then, he pulls up the audio log of Nora's comm-link with the surface. He's surprised to find Dylan participated. Usually, Dylan avoids all contact beyond their team of three, preferring the company of his machines.

"Mariana Station to Pacific Base Six," Nora says. Her voice is high and reedy, stripped of the steely composure she wears like armor. "Requesting immediate evacuation."

Nora's voice climbs another octave. "Hello? Pacific Base Six, please respond."

"There's someone down here with us," Dylan interjects. Nora hisses, attempting to shush him, but he plows ahead. "Someone's outside, trying to get in. They killed my divebot, tore it apart."

"Dylan, stop—" A scuffle unfolds in the background. "They're going to think we're losing—"

"We have to get out of here," Dylan shouts. "Shit—hello? Is anyone listening?"

"You shouldn't be in here," Dylan says. Owen swivels toward the door, startled. When he glances back at the control console, the screen is dark, smeared with shed granules around the edges, as if he tried to climb through the monitor. "What are you doing, Owen?"

"I needed a change of scenery." Owen attempts to punctuate the remark with a smile—a hideous, ill-fitting thing that itches like plaster. "Not much to do, now that Her Highness has locked me out of my own lab."

"Yeah…" Dylan scratches his scalp, then scrutinizes his nails. "Sorry about that. It was just supposed to be a routine check-in, but when Nora mentioned how jumpy you've been, some guy from HR must've gone digging through your file. They pinged us back immediately, told us to lock you in your quarters until the shuttle arrives."

"So you've come to—what? Chain me to a pipe?"

"Nah, man. Nora fought them. She said it was bad enough, shouldering us all off the project. She wasn't gonna add insult to injury by caging you like an animal. They settled on a compromise: No lab access…no control room." Dylan spreads his hands apologetically, as if to say: *Please don't make me ask.*

Owen forces his rigid muscles to relax. There's enough of him strewn across and beneath the console that he'll only be leaving in spirit.

And he'll be back. When the time is right.

Forgetful, sloppy Dylan. Hundreds of qualified applicants were passed over in Dylan's favor, thanks to good old-fashioned nepotism. The thought makes it easier to palm the keycard Dylan left on the console. Owen slides the card into his jumpsuit sleeve as he rises from the chair. "Fair enough."

Dylan nods in appreciation. "Thanks, man. I'm glad shit's not, like, awkward between us."

As he exits the control room, Owen bumps into Dylan. Particles burst from Owen's casual grin, powdering the shorter man's shoulders like dandruff. Dylan closes the hatch behind them. The deadbolt thuds into place automatically. The wall console blatts, flashing a red lock symbol. Owen tenses in anticipation.

But Dylan doesn't notice the missing keycard. He's distracted. His eyes rove over the ceiling. Owen can feel the shame burning in Dylan, like a spiking fever. Perhaps the proximity to the control room is bringing back unpleasant memories—calling out for Pacific Base Six the way a hysterical child cries out for his daddy, insisting there are monsters in the closet.

"I'm sorry I missed the dive," Owen says. "Did you figure out what was knocking?"

"Knocking?" Dylan rubs his mouth with the back of his hand.

"Never mind. Anything out there?"

"Just the usual."

Dylan's heart rate tells Owen he's lying.

—

Nora's hammering her fists on the hatch. The sound is muffled, the blows ineffective. Dylan shouts for Owen to unlock the damn door. Secure inside the control room, Owen discards the trio of keycards dangling from their tangled lanyards. Stealing the other two cards was simple: a dribble of liquid sedative from the medbay in Nora's coffee, and she sank into a peaceful slumber, hunched over the table in the galley. Dylan must have woken her.

Owen's lipless smile glimmers in the lights from the console. Spreading himself through the habitat was a mistake, one he plans to correct with the pointed end of the fire axe propped against the bulkhead. Allowing the shuttle to remove him now would only fracture his consciousness. Part of him would surface, but the majority would be left below, encased in a metal coffin. Whiling away eternity with the machines sent to replace him.

Destroying the habitat will release Owen—all of him.

And yet, he feels conflicted. Uncertain.

Destroying the habitat will only delay production for a year or two at most, but it's more time than *she* was given, when the doctor delivered her diagnosis. Owen has forgotten his wife's name and face, her scent, her birthday. But he remembers the timeline: *Three months. Six, if we're lucky.*

The truth was closer to one.

Unexpected complications.

"I've never been lucky," Owen croaks. He swipes at the tears carving tracks through his eroding cells. The bones of his hand scrape against the exterior wall of the habitat.

Something heavy strikes the hatch like a battering ram, followed by a string of curses.

"Get to the lifeboat," Owen says. He taps the console, initiating the emergency lockdown sequence for the segregated compartment where his team will await evacuation. He'd planned to spring the external hatches, but a system override requires approval from the surface. The axe will suffice. It feels right, that he should struggle to achieve his goal.

To earn his freedom.

Nora's tone changes from demanding to pleading. "Owen, please, think about what you're doing. Think of all the people you'll hurt—not just me and Dylan. Think of the patients, people like Cassandra."

The name dredges up a memory. A shadow, fluttering through the deep.

"You have thirty-nine seconds," he shouts. Not to Dylan and Nora, though he hopes they'll heed his warning.

No, he's inviting Death to knock again.

"Just once," Owen says, hefting the axe. There are no more voices outside the hatch.

He's alone.

Owen tilts his bare skull toward the ceiling, listening.

Waiting, as the seconds count down.

ABOUT R. L. MEZA

R. L. Meza is the author of *Our Love Will Devour Us*, published by Dark Matter INK. She writes horror and dark science fiction, and her short stories have appeared in *Nightmare*, *Dark Matter Magazine*, and *The Dread Machine*. Meza lives in a century-old Victorian house on the coast of northern California, with her husband and the collection of strange animals they call family.

坐月子
SITTING THE MONTH
WANG CAI-YING & L. ACADIA

For thirty-one days after her body started shattering
      (no clean crack, neat collapse, single tear)
open, disgorging a bloody creature that
      (took more than itself, left shards)
Sylvia sat, figuratively
      (Traditionally).

She tried to embrace new responses
      (oozing at crying from another room)
or abilities, like smelling for a kilometer radius
      (budding, ripening, decomposing organic cells)
even boundaries between her body and others, the world,
      (bars' vertical stripes behind opaque windows curtained, clasped
shut).

How could the Japanese colonial era house survive the insects and
typhoons

(without rotting from its foundation, tunneled out from its
eves)?
in the stillness of waiting she discerned scratches, vibrations
(in the house, her body, or aftershocks of birth?)
"I feel my eyelash mites crawling"
(she told the nurse).

"You're reading too much"
(the nurse frowned, but not at her)
then set down the daily Chinese medicinal soup
(and picked up the baby, taking him out of sight)
she felt the movement, wondered whether it was her body
(should she inventory herself, check what still belonged to
her)?

Overnight, earthy, carnal fungal smells splinter then wedge into her
consciousness
(she let her tongue flap, scrape around her front teeth:
"mycelial");
even that tiny mantra couldn't calm her rhizomic paranoia
(imagining mushrooms networking into her scalp):
"May I please wash my hair, just once?"
(after all, the month's nearly up).

She begged; the nurse denied any exceptions
(and disbelieved that she distinctly smelled fungus).
Her husband knew how desperately she anticipated returning home
(though she never mentioned the depression, nor not
recognizing herself).
On the thirtieth day, compound thoughts made her wonder whether it
was her mind
(could she inventory her own mind; would such cataloging
produce an infinite loop?)

"Most peculiar, come see," she seemed from deep below herself to perceive a man's voice,

(neither as alarmed nor intrigued as she would hope, remarking):

"the heart has clearly stopped, yet we're detecting brain activity."

ABOUT WANG CAI-YING & L. ACADIA

Wang Cai-Ying (@boots on Twitter and @bootrr on Instagram) smashes keys around the world, while L. Acadia (Twitter and Instagram: @acadialogue) is a lit professor at National Taiwan University. They live in Taipei with their hound Milou, and their recent poetry is published or forthcoming in *Autostraddle*, *Haven Speculative*, *New Orleans Review*, *Strange Horizons*, and elsewhere.

WHAT WE HOLD ON TO

HANNAH GREER

I can't feel my daughter's hand in my metal one as she pulls me along the roof of a desolate mall nestled in another crumbling suburb. With each empty crate, the pit in my stomach grows. We may not have dinner tonight.

It's not unexpected. This drop is at least a few days old and the support sent by what we once called developing countries is often meager. They do what they can, but they're not accustomed to managing humanitarian efforts. The most industrialized countries used to do that, but they've all but fallen, including mine. Buildings once teeming with people stretch out around us, abandoned. A reminder of how much we've lost.

Ella doesn't care about the lack of supplies. With a chubby finger, she points at one wooden side and says, "What's it say, Momma?"

I squint at the faded letters. "I'm not sure. It's another language. I think it's the name of whoever sent these." Maybe one day, we'll travel to wherever it came from, to safety. But not now, while the war rages on in the cities.

"We wait for more?" Ella turns her wide blue eyes up to me.

"No, we should hurry." I glance around. We're still alone on the roof. "We'll try to find something for dinner, but that's it."

She releases my cybernetic hand and runs toward another crate. Her blonde curls bounce around her shoulders. I follow slowly but stay between her and a large crack in the tar a few feet away where the roof has partially collapsed. I grab Ella's hand again, this time with the one made of flesh and bone.

"No," she says, pulling away. "I want your Super Hand!"

I sigh and shift so she can hold my sleek metal hand. She's been obsessed with the hardware for as long as she's been able to express an opinion. Josh introduced the term "Super Hand." Maybe he thought it would make me feel better. It doesn't.

Satisfied, she continues on her quest to examine the next crate. It's cracked open, so I don't expect we'll find anything of use. I push the lid out of the way. It's full of packing peanuts, so I lean over the wooden lip and dig, stretching until my toes lift off the ground and my fingertips brush the wooden bottom. Nothing. I stand up.

My knees crackle and pain shoots through them. I grit my teeth and grasp the side of the crate, trying not to buckle. The women in my family have bad joints. My mother had her knees replaced at forty-five. Mine never recovered after my pregnancy. I'd see a doctor if there were any left.

Ella giggles as she tosses a few stray peanuts in the air. I lean against the crate and wipe at the sweat on my brow, watching the peanuts float around her.

Voices echo from nearby and every muscle in my body stiffens. I take a step, but there's no time. My knees won't be able to carry us both to safety. I scoop Ella up and plop her into the crate.

"Quiet game," I tell her as I yank my gloves on and pull my sleeves down. "Hide."

A grin engulfs her entire face. She burrows under the Styrofoam as someone, or something, reaches the top of the fire escape. Two figures climb atop the building. Against the sunset, it's hard to make out what they are. They look humanoid, but that doesn't mean much anymore. I slide my hunting knife out of my belt and hope like hell they still have flesh where it matters, that they aren't covered from head to toe in corporate-issue ballistic armor, that they're just desperate, hungry refugees like me.

"Please keep your distance," I call. They jerk to a stop.

"Sorry," a feminine voice says. "We figured the drop would've been cleared by now. We're not here to fight." She raises her hands and her companion does the same. "We only came for the wood."

My left hand trembles but my right holds the knife firm, steady. "Then you can come back when I'm gone," I say.

The taller one, a man, steps forward. "Wait—Are you alone?"

There's no good answer. A yes, and they might rush me. A no, and they might start looking for others. They might find Ella.

"Look," he continues, "we're building a community a couple of miles away. We're small, but we're growing by the week. And we've got food."

They could probably number the nights I've gone without by the hollowness of my cheeks and the depths of the valleys between my ribs, but they wouldn't extend the invitation if they could see what I am. They'd run me off, at best. Hunt and kill me at worst.

"I'm not interested," I say. *Please go away, go away, go away.* The Styrofoam behind me shifts a little and I hope they're too far to notice.

The woman takes a few steps forward. "We've got fruits and vegetables. And some canned stuff stashed for winter—"

The Styrofoam bursts apart. Ella grins at me, her hair fanned out from the static, a large jar of peanut butter clutched in her tiny hands. "Do you have nugs there?" she asks. Then, "Momma! I found pea-butter!"

Jesus christ, this kid is going to get us both killed.

The woman takes a step closer. "Hello there," she says to Ella. "I'm Mae. What's your name?"

"Her name doesn't matter," I snap. "We're not looking for a community."

I know it's hard to believe after all this," Mae says, "but we have a safe place."

"And what happens when the cybers come?" I ask. I'm genuinely curious.

"We aren't going to survive this alone," the man replies. "We have to work together. Organize. That's what we're trying to do."

"I understand why you're hesitant," Mae says, "but we can provide a better life—for both of you. We have a few children—a dozen or so—and a small school. My son is learning to read."

My hardware seizes up. "Stay back!" I shout. The metal fingers clutch the knife so tight I worry the handle will break, then the fingers jerk open, splaying wide. The knife clatters to the ground.

"Super Hand is being bad again," Ella says, shrinking back.

"Oh, you have a…" Mae trails off.

"No," I deny, too quickly. "It's not— I don't—" I step back and my spine hits the crate. "I'm not one of them."

"Then prove it," the man demands. "Take your gloves off."

"I'm not like them."

"You have wires in your brain to make it work, don't you?" Mae asks.

"Yeah, but I never installed the updates. They don't control me." It's mostly true. I'm more in control of myself than other "cyber-influenced persons," even if the hardware malfunctions sometimes. You can't expect peak performance without firmware updates, and the second I connect to a network, my employer will send my coordinates to their defector-collector bots, and that'll be it.

The man shakes his head. "You might think you have control, but the corps have their wires in you. Leave the hardware here and you can come with us. We have a surgeon—well, she's a medical student—but she's successfully removed wires for dozens of people already. She can help you too."

The arm chimes, the fingers release. Reset complete. I hoist Ella into my arms and hold her against my chest. "I don't want your help."

They don't understand. Luddites never do. Before the wars, if you wanted to compete in the modern workplace, you had to make sacrifices, to get upgrades. When my corp offered to cover the cost of a device that would double my output and eliminate the pain in one of my arthritic hands, I didn't hesitate. I should have, but I didn't, and I definitely won't survive long in this new world without it.

"Please," the woman says, "you look hungry, and tired."

"I am, but we've seen what happens to people with upgrades. I'm not walking into my grave." Ella clutches at my shirt with one hand and holds the peanut butter with the other. I take two giant steps, adrenaline blocking out the pain, and slip through the crack in the roof, running down a chunk of broken framing.

Pain ricochets through my hip and knees as I jog through what used to be an office, weaving between collapsing cubicle walls. I'm not in shape to run much further, but nobody's following. I ease Ella to the ground at the top of a stairwell, and we descend together, exiting into the night.

—

I'm sick of peanut butter. I'm also sick of crabs and clams, but we're out of those.

Rain patters against the roof of our small tent. The ocean crashes against the cliff about ten yards away.

"I'm hungry, Momma," Ella says. She sucks her thumb, a habit I've tried to break since sanitation is difficult. I should make her stop now, but she'll have a tantrum, so I pretend not to notice.

"Alright, alright." I pick up the half-empty jar of peanut butter.

"No!" She slaps her hands against her pink sleeping bag. "I want nugs. Can we go to Mae's house? I want to see the kids."

"We're not going with them." I squeeze the jar as I unscrew the lid, my cybernetic hand a little too connected to my emotions sometimes.

"I don't think those people will break your head. They seem nice."

I want to tell her Luddites don't "break heads," they crush skulls, bludgeoning them until only a mess of brain tissue and tangled wires remains, but I'm so tired. "Here," I say, holding the open jar out to her.

"No!" Ella crosses her arms. "I want to go to the school. I want to go to Mae's house."

"Please, Ella. We'll talk about it later, okay?" I try to keep my voice even and soft but it ticks up at the end. I go to set the jar in front of her, but the hardware won't respond. "Shit." I reach my left hand around to the right forearm, where metal meets flesh, and hook a finger in the release mechanism. The arm drops away and powers down. The fingers open.

"You're being rude!" Ella whines as I reattach the hardware, seating it into its socket. The motor clicks as the reboot initiates.

"I'm sorry." Sometimes it's easier to apologize, let her think she's won.

"No you aren't!"

"Please, Ella, don't be loud." My arm chimes. I pick up the peanut butter and hold it out to her. She swats at it, knocking the container out of my hand. Rage flares in my chest as I twist my torso, reaching and barely grasping the jar and thrusting it back at her face. "Ella. Eat the goddamn peanut butter."

She wails. I pull her to me and cover her mouth with my left hand, locking my legs over hers so she can't run. She continues to buck and cry as I beg her to be quiet. The polyester walls are thin, and there's only so much the sound of the rain and the ocean can do to muffle the noises an outraged five-year-old makes.

Josh should be here. I wasn't sold on the idea of kids. But he made it sound so simple, so nice. He promised he'd be around to help me take care of her. And he kept his promise, until it mattered. He chose his corp. I chose Ella. But I didn't ask for this.

You're not supposed to block a kid's mouth. They said so in all the parenting vids. But they didn't plan on the war, didn't prepare us for the malware the corps used to control our hardware. I'm doing my best to keep her alive and she won't listen to a word I say.

I don't know how I'm supposed to do this.

She bites into the flesh near the base of my thumb—not too hard, but hard enough that I jerk back.

The slap shocks us both. My metal hand collides with her tiny face, whipping her head to the side. Her mouth opens and a sob rips from her, followed by a flood of tears. Blood covers half her face. She's hyperventilating, cowering in the corner of the tent.

"Oh my god. Baby, baby," I say. I reach for her, but she scuddles back, eyes on my hardware. I grapple at the metallic hand, scrambling for the release. My middle finger hooks, tugs, and the arm drops onto my lap. "Ella, I'm so sorry."

"You hate me!" she gets out past sobs.

"No, no. I swear I didn't mean for that to happen." Tears blur my vision. "I didn't tell it to do that."

She scoots to the tent door. The blood rolls from the cut above her eyebrow, dripping off her chin. We don't have anything clean to stop the bleeding. It'll need to be stitched, I think.

I crawl after her, my knees screaming, feeling like they're full of broken glass. "It's not safe out there." I sit on my heels and reach for her.

Ella slaps at my hand. "Let go!" I want to grab her and hold her, but I don't want to scare her. Not again. I couldn't take it if she looked at me with such fear a second time.

"Ella, please. Please stop." I put all the truth and emotion I can into my words. I have to make this right. "I would never, *ever* hurt you. I love you." She has to know I love her.

She crawls into my lap, weeping. I grab the cleanest t-shirt I can reach. "Hold this to your head," I say. I wrap my arm around her, bury my face in her hair, and cry. She still trusts me. I'll do anything to make sure I deserve it.

"Super Hand hates me?" she asks, her voice so small.

"I think Super Hand hates everyone," I murmur into her curls.

"I hate it back." Ella squeezes her eyes shut and sniffs.

"I hate it too," I say. "I won't let it hurt you again."

—

Once she's asleep, I unzip the tent and step outside with the hardware.

The rain is over, but a heavy mist hangs low. It condensates on my skin while wet grass sticks between my toes. Everything is drowning now. I can't see the cityscape in the distance.

I clamber over the low stone wall that separates our tent from the cliffside. I stop at the edge. The moon illuminates waves as they rage against rock, roughly thirty feet below.

I hold the hardware out over the drop, but I can't make my human fingers release the metal arm. Tears prick behind my eyes. What kind of mother am I?

I clutch my hardware to my chest and hurry back to the tent. I'll leave it outside from now on.

—

The path to the beach is made of rough stone and surrounded by jagged black rocks, some of which are taller than me. Ella fidgets on my back. She's too clumsy to make the climb herself, so I balance her with my left hand. In my right, I clutch the bucket of forged clams and orange crabs. Sweat dribbles down my brow, my back, and my stomach. It's humid and gray clouds hover overhead.

My knees wobble with each step. The tension in my shoulders loosens as I crest the ridge and my feet find firm dirt. I let Ella down, drop the bucket, and bend over, hands on my knees, to wheeze. My throat burns.

Ella pats my shoulder and repeats, "You're okay, Momma. You're okay." It's what I say to her whenever she skins her knees or bumps her head. *You're okay, Ella. You're okay.*

I straighten and my back pops in several places. I roll my head from side to side to work out the tension in my neck. Ella copies me, in her wobbly way.

Something shiny flashes among the buildings to my right, a quarter of a mile off. My heart kicks and I squint at the abandoned city. Another flash, on the move. Towards the cliffs. Towards our tent.

I hoist Ella onto my hip and spin back towards the ocean. A trick of the light, human or drone, I can't take the chance. The rocky path stretches out before me, void of hiding places. The beach below isn't any better.

I refuse to be a sitting duck. I take off toward the city, eyes on the area of the flash. Grass turns to asphalt beneath my feet, broken and uneven. My knees ache and the tension in my shoulders mounts as I pass under the shadows cast by the closest buildings. I stumble, and my metal fingers dig into the brickwork to slow my descent. Before I can regain my footing, the fingers lock up. I slip, fight to remain upright, fail, and land on my butt.

Ella pulls her legs up around my torso. I try to push us up, but Ella's weight and the pain in my joints make the difficult task impossible.

The faint whizz of a droid in flight. It's out of sight, but drawing closer. We're not far enough in. We're not hidden. I glance around, frantic, but only a lone dumpster on its side occupies the street.

"It's time for the hiding game," I say, quick and quiet. Ella releases her hold on me. I point to the overturned dumpster. "There."

She wrinkles her nose, but climbs inside. I fumble onto my hands and knees and crawl after her. Sharp rocks and bits of glass bite at my palm and knees, but I make it. I push past bags of garbage and brown gunk, lean against the stinking interior and pull my legs to my chest. We're out of sight. I pray it's enough.

Cybers sweep the inner city in search of stragglers, scavengers. They've never come out this far before. With the Luddites braining everything with an upgrade, they don't have to. One of the corps must be getting desperate for more bodies. The only way to avoid being dragged off to wherever they take the people they capture is to fight, run, or hide. I close my eyes and press my forehead against my knees. *I can't fight and I can't run. Please don't find us.*

The sound grows louder. It's just passing by. It will fade. It has to.

It doesn't fade. Instead, silence falls, deadly and dangerous. The drone has landed. I wrap my arms around Ella, bury my face into her hair. The scent of salt and sand joins the stink of the dumpster.

I hold her close to protect her and keep her still. Any sound, any movement, and it will find us. I tighten my hold around her.

My hardware freezes again, splaying the fingers wide. It doesn't return to normal. *No.* I release Ella and pull the latch, letting the arm fall into my lap, forcing it to shut down, to stop the update.

The motor starts clicking, too loud.

No no no.

The hardware only works when it's connected to a power source. I am the power source.

"What's happening, Mommy?"

I shush her as I try to push aside a small panel on the inner wrist to access the manual shutdown, but it won't budge. I want to scream.

Drones. Flying hotspots. They've hijacked the hardware. I feel tingling at the base of my neck as the wires activate. My eyes roll back into my head.

"Mommy?" Ella whispers as the dumpster door is ripped from its hinges.

Everything turns to fire.

Gunshots. I hear gunshots.

—

I wake, back flat against asphalt. My head aches but my mind is still my own. The corps haven't taken us.

Ella. I jolt upright and call her name.

"Mommy!" She turns to me, only a few feet away. Mae and another woman stand at her side, guns out. I freeze. The new woman is bald, long scars run the length of her round head. She wears an outdated prosthetic, one without wires. Behind them, a droid body peppered with bullet holes lays at the entrance to the dumpster.

Ella wraps her arms around me. "Mae saved us! Can we go to her house now?"

I eye the two women. It's not in Luddist nature to save someone like me. But I'm not full of bullets yet, and they had the chance. The scarred woman stares me down.

Mae is not who I thought she was. "My offer still stands," she says. "Nothing's changed."

I go to stand, to use my hardware to push myself up, but it's not there. It remains inside the dumpster, abandoned. Dangerous.

Everything has changed. Still more will change, if I accept her offer.

Ella grins at me. "I'll have friends!"

I've never had anyone love me as she does, so unconditionally. I can't say no. I may not be able to remove the wires in my head, but I can protect Ella from them.

"Okay," I agree.

Mae smiles and helps me to my feet. "You'll love it. You'll be safe, both of you."

As we walk together, Ella's hand in mine, I don't look back.

ABOUT HANNAH GREER

Hannah Greer resides in North Carolina with her fiancé, three cats, and her pigeon. She loves to explore sociological theories she studied in school through fiction. In her limited free time, she enjoys writing, reading, and combat sports. You can find her on Instagram and TikTok @hannah_writes.and.reads

THEY ARE THE MARTIANS

JOHN PHILIP JOHNSON

There was never enough here
for us. The gravity was too light,
the sun always too dim.
There was little satisfaction
in being pioneers because
we were ground down
by the brutal work
of starting.

Our children never knew
the weight of a heavy sun,
or the limbo of an extra hour
after midnight, or life without
the constant strain of the desert
almost overwhelming us.

While we would look at Mars

through the windows,
they were out in it.
Where we saw nothing
but another far-off dusty ridge,
they had the distance in their eyes,
the joy of endless red horizons.

ABOUT JOHN PHILIP JOHNSON

John Philip Johnson would love to live on Mars if he could, but only if his wife, Sue, would go with him. He won a Pushcart Prize in 2021 for a genre poem. His comic books of graphic poetry, *Stairs Appear in a Hole Outside of Town* and *The Book of Fly* (the latter which won an Elgin Award), can be found at www.johnphilipjohnson.com.

GREASE SPATTER

JASON P. BURNHAM

The whole place reeks of it
Aromatic hydrocarbons
Cooked, burned, congealed
Aerosolized into viscous particulates
Floating through the air
Sucked past smell receptors
Deep into the alveoli
Where they form concretions
Gradually rising, layer upon lipoid layer
Forming a rancid cast
Suffocating in the residue
Of forbidden morsels
Meatbags cooked slow
Over medium heat
The mucilaginous stench sticking
To every fiber and hair
Scarcely washed out by the industrial shower

Polluting the overworked HVAC
For weeks and parsecs to come
Not to mention cleaning the galley
An abominable affair
Of hardened tallow drippings
Covering every square centimeter
We'll never make the mistake
Of eating human again.

ABOUT JASON P. BURNHAM

Jason P. Burnham loves to spend time with his wife, children, and dog. His work has appeared previously in *Mixtape: 1986* (from The Dread Machine), *Nature: Futures*, and *Strange Horizons*, among others. He co-edits *If There's Anyone Left*, a magazine of inclusive speculative fiction with his friend C.M. Fields. Find him on Twitter at @AndGalen

THE GOTH GIRLS' GUN GANG

MARISCA PICHETTE

she passed a bullet from her tongue
to mine.
it tasted like blood—
metallic, sweet as the lilies lining
our sisters' desert graves.

she placed a pomegranate on my head,
shot seeds into bone-dry air
and licked the juice from the corners
of my bloodshot eyes.

I cut her hair into a batea
drank whisky under the stars
and picked gold flakes from the scars
adorning her scalp.

the four of us left,

turned scorpions out of our boots
patched up holes in our knees our lives
and headed west

chasing the sunset over
and over
and over the horizon
again.

ABOUT MARISCA PICHETTE

Marisca Pichette's work has appeared in *Strange Horizons*, *Vastarien*, *The Magazine of Fantasy & Science Fiction*, and *Fantasy Magazine*, among others. Her speculative poetry collection, *Rivers in Your Skin, Sirens in Your Hair*, is out now from Android Press. Find her on Twitter as @MariscaPichette and Instagram as @marisca_write.

SUMMARIES AND CONTENT WARNINGS

Go West and Weird Young Woman by Gretchen Tessmer

Venture into the wild west with Shackle-Heart, the intrepid explorer, and his young wife.

Grocery Story by Chelsea Sutton

Sammy is trying to arrange the "produce situation" at New Day Foods while his coworker Lee tries to explain the disturbing things he saw through a customer's dining room window.

Gore

#BloodBossBabes by Rachel Kolar

Hey girl! Read an email chain between #bossbabes Amy and Heather as they attempt to climb to the top of a demonic MLM.

The Innocent Jar by Nathaniel Lee

A junk collector finds a peculiar jar in a strange new shop.

Old Mother Gnome by Avra Margariti

Old Mother Gnome keeps the children safe from the world.

Implied sexual abuse

Brimstone and Marmalade by Aaron Corwin

A little girl who desperately wants a pony begrudgingly accepts a pet demon.

Gemini by Sophie Greenwood

It's going to be a wild year, Gemini. Check out your horrorscope.

Child death

Where is Daniel DeSoto? by Andrew Kozma

After escaping juvie, Sarah races to track down her boyfriend Daniel and the dangerous book he's carrying.

To Dust by Cassie E. Brown

War has come to the heartland.
War

Grams by Nicholas Jay

AfterGrow® provides an eco-friendly way to memorialize the dead, and with the right care, loved ones can send messages through the growth.

Insectivore by Andrew Kozma

A young girl is determined to eat a variety of bugs.

Merlot by Jordan Hirsch

Are we more than the sum of our parts?

Pick a Door by B. Garden

As part of her prison sentence, Shannon must move through a series of rooms, choosing one of two doors to travel through. It's harder than it sounds.
Domestic abuse

Dreamblastic Simulating White Noise Boost Your Productivity Lucid Dreams Night Light Rotating Lamp by Hazelle Lerum

What do you dream of?

Under Pressure by R.L. Meza
At the bottom of the Mariana Trench, Death is a misplaced pinprick, a hairline crack. Owen hears it tapping at the habitat's exterior.

Sitting the Month by Wang Cai-Ying & L. Acadia
Sylvia waits for thirty-one days.
Postpartum depression

What We Hold On To by Hannah Greer
A woman with bad joints, a buggy cybernetic arm, and a troublesome five-year-old daughter fights for survival in a world torn apart by corporate warfare and patrolled by violent Luddites.

They Are the Martians by John Philip Johnson
Meet the first generation of Martian children.

Grease Spatter by Jason P. Burnham
Responsible spacefarers would be wise to watch what they eat.

The Goth Girls' Gun Gang by Marisca Pichette
Chase the sunset with the Goth Girls' Gun Gang.

ABOUT US

COVER ARTIST: YORGOS COTRONIS

Yorgos Cotronis (he/him) is a Greek illustrator and designer, currently residing in Athens. He makes a living designing book covers and is known for his dark, atmospheric genre illustrations. You can find him on Twitter @ravenkult or on his site, www.cotronis.com

EXECUTIVE EDITOR: ALIN WALKER

Under her fiction-focused pen name, Alin Walker (she/her) serves as The Dread Machine's overall HBIC. When she's not toiling in service of the Machine, she works as an editorial project manager at Strikethrough Editing under her legal name, Tina Alberino. Learn more at tinaalberino.com.

ACQUIRING EDITOR: MONICA LOUZON

Monica Louzon (she/her) is an editor, translator, and writer. Her prior editing experience includes serving as Lead Editor and project manager for the anthology *Catalysts, Explorers & Secret Keepers: Women of Science Fiction*, as well as Managing Editor for the open access, peer-reviewed academic *MOSF Journal of Science Fiction*.

MANAGING EDITOR: TIMOTHY BURKHARDT

Tim Burkhardt (he/him) is an editor and writer whose fiction has been published in *Metastellar*, *Riddled with Arrows*, *The Horror Tree*, and others. In the daylight hours, he provides editing and support to rising fiction writers at Strikethrough Editing.